Y0-EIH-722

DISCARD

W FIC RED
Redding, Robert H.
  Tucker's law

92096099

TUCKER'S LAW

Other books by Robert H. Redding:

McCall
Steele
Londagin

TUCKER'S LAW
•
Robert H. Redding

AVALON BOOKS
NEW YORK

© Copyright 2005 by Robert H. Redding
All rights reserved.
All the characters in this book are fictitious,
and any resemblance to actual persons,
living or dead, is purely coincidental.
Published by Thomas Bouregy & Co., Inc.
160 Madison Avenue, New York, NY 10016

Library of Congress Cataloging-in-Publication Data

Redding, Robert H.
  Tucker's law / Robert H. Redding.
     p. cm.
  ISBN 0-8034-9751-2
  1. Revenge—Fiction. 2. Cattle drives—Fiction. 3. Cattle stealing—Fiction. I. Title.

PS3568.E336T83   2006
813'.54—dc22

2005021964

PRINTED IN THE UNITED STATES OF AMERICA
ON ACID-FREE PAPER
BY HADDON CRAFTSMEN, BLOOMSBURG, PENNSYLVANIA

Chapter One

Brad Tucker felt the danger. He couldn't see anything, because the Kansas night was black as tar, but his nerves twanged. He'd been through several scrapes in his twenty-eight years and knew what his present tension meant.

"You feel it?" he asked his companion, a shadowy figure in the moonless dark.

"Yep."

"Me too," responded another voice, a young voice, maybe fifteen or sixteen years old.

"Better alert the boys, Stace," said Brad. The first figure turned his horse toward the herd.

"Let's get some coffee," muttered Brad.

The remaining pair returned to the chuck

wagon. Cooky Belton had a fire blazing. A gray pot nestled among the hot coals of the fire's outer edges. Brad poured a tin cup for the youth and one for himself.

Cooky, a skinny man with a face so wrinkled the crew gave him another nickname, "Prune," appeared. He wiped his hands on a stained, white apron.

"Git 'em bedded down, Brad?" he asked in a raspy too-much-trail-dust voice.

Brad nodded, and sipped.

"How much more we gotta go?"

"About thirty miles to the Smoky Hill River, Prune."

"Three days there, you reckon?"

"And two more to Abilene."

"I can't wait," cut in the youngest one of the trio. He was red-headed, and his hair shined in the firelight. He grinned. "My first real pay coming." He smacked his fist into the palm of his hand. "Hey, I'll have me a time."

Brad Tucker grinned. He'd been young once—a thousand years ago? He remembered his first pay, and how he was fleeced in a poker game by card sharks.

"Be careful," he cautioned. "Bad ones want your money."

"Ah, I can take care of myself," was the assured retort.

Brad remembered the scared youngster he'd taken under his wing in a backtrail cowtown. Red, that was all the name he gave, was broke, dirty, starving, and a runaway from a drunken home. He had no horse. To be without a horse in cow country was akin to being without feet. Where could you go without a horse? How to find work on a ranch? Red, in fact, had nothing at all, expect for the clothes on his back, if the tatters he wore could be called clothes.

He'd boldly approached Brad on the street and asked for a job. Brad had sized the boy up, and gave him credit for his move, and then had hired him. Ever since, he had taken a liking to the kid. There was an air about him that demanded attention.

Brad had loaned the boy a horse, advanced him pay so he could buy decent clothes, a bedroll, and a pistol. The weapon wasn't for defense, but for herding cattle. The noise of the firearm sent the animals in the right direction.

"We have a thousand mile drive to Abilene," Brad remembered telling the youth, "with EW cattle. Think you can keep up?"

And Red, who hadn't an ounce of experience at anything much at all, had flashed back with the confidence of ignorance, "By the time we get there, I'll be your trail boss."

Brad hadn't been let down. Red was

inexperienced, but he worked his skinny butt off. He liked what he was doing and learned fast. He still couldn't be put to night-hawking, guarding the cattle after dark, a job that required experienced hands, but Brad was pleased to note the boy was coming along.

Stace worked his way out of the shadows. He was a slim man, average height, but well-proportioned, and he moved smoothly like water over stones. In the daylight, the observer saw sandy hair, and light blue eyes, which turned steely if the occasion called for it.

"The boys are ready," he said and poured coffee. He swallowed and winced.

"Prune," he scoffed, "a horse I used to own could make better gargle than this."

"Make yer own then," was the lively response, "I ain't got no objection."

Stace gave a disdainful grunt, and squatted by the fire. He'd done his duty. If you didn't give the cook a bad time now and then, the man who wrangled the groceries felt abused. Prune was probably one of the best cooks on the Plains, but there wasn't anybody who would tell him that; that would be breaking the rules. Stace was a man who followed the rules. He allowed a thin smile in the shadows. Well, most of the time. He followed rules all right, most of the time.

Brad Tucker said nothing during this exchange, but he nodded in satisisfaction. All was in order. Stace was another oddball he'd picked up. He'd come across him fighting five others in a cowtown down the trail. Didn't seem fair, so he waded in to help. In minutes the five were hightailing it down the street. Tucker was six foot two inches tall and two hundred pounds in dry boots. One of his men said the boss was so hard he could split wood with his eyebrows.

After the two had brushed the fight dust off, Stace stuck out his hand, and said right off, "I'm broke and need a job." He had paused, thought a moment, then added, "I got a record and spent jail time."

Brad sized the man up carefully. Anybody who would take on five men alone deserved a hearing.

"What you spend time in jail for?"

"Self-defense."

"You killed somebody?"

"You ever hear of the Buck ranch range war?"

Everybody had heard of the battle for water rights.

Brad nodded.

"Well, our side lost, and I got locked up."

"You break out?"

"Nah, they let me go after a couple of years. Some kind of a pardon, because I shot in self-defense. Takes the law a long time to get things straight sometimes."

Brad noticed stace carried two .45 pearl-handled pistols. Both were slung low on his hips. Only a certain kind of man carried his weapons thus, a man with guns for hire.

"We don't want trouble on the trail," Brad said. "We got enough trouble getting three thousand cows to Abilene."

"I paid my debt to so-cie-ty," was the ironic response. "You won't get trouble from me."

"Who were those men?"

"Leftovers from the range war. They wanted me to gang up with them. I said no." He grinned, and touched a swollen lip where a hostile knuckle had landed. "They took exception."

"Well, one of our men quit the other day. You're hired, but the first sign of trouble, and you draw your pay. Understood? What's your handle?"

"Stace" was the only name Brad got.

Nothing more was said about either the fight, or Stace's time in jail. He proved to be a good hand. He knew punching and wrangling, as did most men long in the west. After a few weeks Brad put him on point, leading the way.

Stace knew how to avoid sink holes, and buck brush, and always managed to halt the cattle in good pasture.

Brad stared at the fire. He didn't know if the coffee was helping his nerves or not. He was responsible for a lot of cattle carrying the EW brand. This was his third trip to Abilene in as many years. He knew the trail and shortcuts that saved time. He was ahead of schedule and was pleased that his work was getting him closer to his goal. Brad Tucker wanted his own spread, and the money he was paid as trail boss, two hundred a month, plus a percentage of the sale price, would get him closer to that goal. Three thousand head would bring a good price, but the cows were thin after two months, so Brad was heading for some grasslands near Abilene. A month's feeding on that would fatten the animals, bringing a nice profit.

But, and this was a big 'but,' matters had gone too easily. On the previous two trips, he'd had trouble. On the first, he lost over fifty head to the sucking quick sands of the Gila River. On the second, a bad storm stampeded the critters. They ran wild for ten miles before they were stopped. Some barged over cliffs and were killed; others got lost and were never seen again. On both trips, he'd been stopped by Indians demanding tribute for passing over their land. That, alone, cost twenty-five a head each time.

This third trip was somehow not right. No trouble. Too smooth. No losses to quicksand, no stampedes, no tributes, and he was ahead of schedule. The cattle would get an extra week's feeding, maybe two if Ed Warshal, the EW owner, gave permission. When they got closer, he'd ride ahead and wire Ed to find out. Ed was a smart business man. Fatter cows, bigger profits. Permission would come.

Brad Tucker found himself listening to the night for strange sounds. Anything other than the soft chants of the night crew lulling the animals would be worth hearing.

Something was in the air. Brad knew himself well enough to realize his tension was not based on imagination. Nerves? After a couple of months on a rugged trail, maybe. But Brad forgave that thought, and continued to listen to the night sounds.

His glance fell on the shadowed figure of Stace.

The man had been good. He knew cattle, but, apparently, he knew about the owl-hoot trail as well, outlawry. His fight with former cohorts, who wanted him to join them in making *real money,* told Brad that. Did Stace have anything to do with the tension he was feeling? Was Stace going to double cross him?

Brad shook the thought clear of his head. He didn't want to think that, but, after all, he'd hired Stace on instinct. Was that good enough? Prune and the others were a bit wall-eyed over the hiring, though they'd said nothing to him.

Giving his mind a rest from the pressured present, Brad allowed himself to recall his own past. He had been close to following the owl-hoot trail himself. After his parents died within a couple of months of each other, his father from blood poisoning, his mother in childbirth during which the infant, a girl, also died, Brad struck out. He left their hard-scrabble ranch in eastern Wyoming and drifted. Being young, eighteen, he had joined easy company, young men like himself, all at loose ends. They robbed a stage coach and enjoyed the quick money. They planned another.

But, first, they'd try rustling, and chose the EW brand as a test. Before they could give their first whoop to get the cattle moving, Ed Warshal himself, along with several hardened cowboys, surprised them. There was a fight, and the gang scattered. There were no injuries, but Brad was captured.

Instead of turning him over to the law, Ed, a big, steady, white-haired man with a handle-bar mustache, stared him down.

"You're no crook," he had decided. "What's up, kid? A bit of fun? That kind of fun could get you hung."

"I was going to steal your cattle." Brad had been surprised by his own honesty. "That makes me a crook."

"No, that makes you a run-by youngster with nothing better to do. You aren't a crook yet."

Brad had remained silent, wondering.

"I was like you once," Ed Warshal had continued, "but I got caught in Lincoln's war and fought for the Union. A war turned me around, so I'm going to give you a chance to get turned around too. Ah, got a name?"

"Brad, Brad Tucker."

"All right, I'm going to give you a job." The owner of the EW balled his fist into knot. "You do well, you stay. If not, you go." His voice had hardened. "Don't ever let me catch you rustling again. Do you understand what I'm saying?"

The almost-outlaw understood perfectly. He had risen in the ranks ever since, becoming a foreman and trail boss. He was good, and his services were in demand by other ranchers. He was offered more money, but he stuck with Ed Warshal. Once he asked his boss, "What can I do to pay you back for saving my worthless life?"

"Just one thing."

"Name it."

"If you see some young man heading for trouble like you were, pass it on."

"Pass it on?"

"Yes. Give him a chance, like I did you."

And so Stace became a member of the crew. He was not a young man, like Red, but Brad sensed an earnestness in Stace. He really wanted to get away from—whatever, whatever it was that prompted him to keep two pistols tied down.

As for Red, at fifteen he hadn't arrived at trouble's door yet. Brad grinned. EW's wish was being filled.

He rose and threw the remainder of his coffee on the fire.

"It's getting about my turn to stand watch. You too, Stace, let's go."

"You could let me come," muttered Red. "I got to learn night work sooner or later."

"Oh, you'll get your chance," Brad told him, "when we hit the grazing fields of Abilene."

"What you mean?" Worry lines crinkled Red's smooth brow.

"I mean you'll stand watch there nearly every night. You'll never want to see a herd of cows again."

"Awww, boss . . . !"

Brad mounted his horse, Smoky. Smoky was a gelding and had owned Brad for five years now. At least that was how Brad felt about the horse. Who owned a horse? A horse had ways of showing who was in charge. The idea always appealed to Brad, and he addressed the animal man-to-horse.

"Let's go, Smoke," and they turned toward the herd.

Brad smiled. He knew what young Red was thinking—he'd be wasting his nights watching cows when he could be whooping it up in Abilene's so called Devil's Addition, where the good times rolled. It was enough to frustrate any fifteen-year-old.

"What do you think of that, Smoke?" he said to his horse, and Smoky's ears perked.

Brad patted the animal's arched neck.

"You couldn't care less, eh? A bale of hay and a bag of oats are all you want, and the ladies can dance on their own, right?"

The horse snorted, as if he understood perfectly.

They drew abreast of the herd, and Hank, the lead man, rode up.

"Everything all right, Hank?"

"Right as frog's hair," was the happy reply. He, too, had expected trouble, and was relieved to see the boss. Even though the night was calm, and the stars bright in the sky, Hank sensed a twist in the scheme of things. He'd been night hawk for many herds and knew when trouble might hit, but the tension on this night was strange, ghostlike, a sensing, rather than a sighting.

He told Brad, "I feel odd, you know? Like something's going to jump on us."

Brad nodded. "Yeah, well, get back to camp for a steak and coffee. Maybe you'll feel better."

Still, Hank's words echoed his own feelings.

He and Stace circled the herd and contacted the rest of the men. Long Jim and Blacky also returned to camp. When they returned, Scarecrow and Jack would get their turn. At two A.M., the four would be relieved so they could sleep. Four others in the crew would take over. Driving a herd meant little sleep, and long hours. As the saying went, "The night's threw the sun out."

"Wonder what's happened to Ruffy?" Stace asked. "He was sent ahead to scout the trail, but should've been back by now."

"Maybe he smelled booze in Abilene,"

grunted Brad, who didn't like being deserted. A couple of his men had done just that at a dinky cowtown a few days before. They'd had enough of the long, long trail. Brad had to scratch to get replacements, not easy in dinky cowtowns.

No sooner had Long Jim and Blacky nudged their ponies toward the fire, than a shot rang out. There were a series of wild yells and more shots. The silhouette of Jack crumpled, and shadowy figures burst out of the gloom. Orange fire bloomed from the muzzles of .45's as the figures charged into the herd.

Brad Tucker reacted instantly. "Rustler's men!" he shouted, and drew his weapon. "Use your guns. We got real trouble!"

And then he felt a bullet crash into his shoulder.

Chapter Two

Earlier that day, several men gathered in an office over Abilene's Alamo Saloon.

"I want that EW herd."

The words came from a smooth-haired man. He smoked a thin Havana cigar. His face was pink and rounded, the result of too much rich food. The fingers holding the thin cigar were also rounded, and pink. Hard labor had never wrinkled their smooth texture. He was dressed in a tailored suit, and his soft calf boots were fashioned by a Houston craftsman. He flicked a long, hot ash to the floor.

"Can you handle it, Ten?"

The man addressed stirred in his chair. He stood up, uncoiling a long, sinewy frame. His hands were large, and hardened. The fingers extending from them were, like the man's body, slender and sinewy. His face was hollowed, with sunken cheeks, and his black eyes glittered in amusement.

"Handle it, Slick? Who else has been doing your dirty work for the past two years?"

"You're well paid for it."

Ten fingered the thonged holster at his side. The pistol in the tooled leather was a .44 Smith and Wesson.

"I earn my pay," he said quietly. He made an effort to smile, but the effort turned into more of a snarl. "You got any regrets, Slick?"

"No! No!"

Slick Comer assumed a bluff and hearty, almost comradely attitude.

"You and your men did well on the GF brand last month. Got nearly every cow in the herd." He returned Ten's effort at a grin. "You do as well tonight, and I'll double your bonus."

Ten nodded. "You'll be along, right?"

"Wouldn't miss it."

The other men in the room remained silent. There was no need for them to speak. Let the two bosses take care of the palaver. The others were present for the details.

Comer addressed them.

"You will each head a small band of men

for your part in this. I think we understand the strategy, do we not?"

One of them, a stocky man, with a scarred, dark face, spoke up.

"We do. We been in on these schemes four times now. We got it pretty well down. We chase the cows to that low wide valley about fifty miles west of town."

"And what next, Sierra?"

"We change brands there."

"Right. It's going to take a lot of work." Slick Comer turned to the others. "About thirty men, like last time for the rustle, and the new brands. Got it?"

The others nodded.

"What's the brand going to be?" Sierra asked.

"Well, me and Ten been giving that some thought. EW ain't easy to change, but we think Box W Bar will do the trick. Make a box out of the E, and cross a leg of the W with a bar."

"Going to take a while, even with a lot of men," said another man. He was a very blond person, blond, combed hair, blond eyebrows, blond skin with sun blotches.

"Not too long, Jord. I got a buyer lined up, and he wants us to get in and out of Abilene fast."

Jord nodded, satisfied. There were no more questions.

Slick continued. "We'll meet at the usual place just after dark. Saddle your strongest and fastest horses. We have a long way to go. The EW herd is now about forty miles south." He smiled. "We can use their horses after we kill off the crew."

The men started to file out.

"And no drinking," cautioned Slick Comer. "We'll need clear heads tonight." He turned to Ten. "Stay a bit, Ten."

The men left, and the first thing they did was pause at the Alamo's bar for a drink. No fancy-suit dude was going to tell them what not to do! True, they'd all worked with Comer, and knew him to be a good schemer; they admired his brains and planning ability, but they condemmed his brass. They would not get drunk, but they would surely have a drink or two.

After the door closed behind them, Ten turned to Comer. "What?"

"That GF job wasn't so good."

"You said it went fine."

"Oh, we got nearly all the cattle all right, and we killed all the men, no witnesses is what we thought, but we were wrong."

"Oh?" Ten's cheeks tightened. He was surprised.

"One person was left. That's dangerous, Ten."

"We got everybody," insisted Ten. He fingered the butt of his pistol. "I ought to know. I made sure them that was wounded was finished."

"You didn't get George Fanchy's daughter."

"The daughter?" Ten's eyebrows lifted in surprise. "We didn't see no woman there."

"She was at the GF ranch."

"Then how could we get her?" Ten's voice grew thin. Being told he was inefficient really raised his ire.

"You couldn't," Comer's voice dropped to a hush for some reason, "but you can get her now. She's in town."

"What harm can she do?" Ten didn't mind killing, business was business, but he didn't go looking to waste lead. "She don't know any of us."

"True, but she's asking questions. She's looking. We killed her Daddy, Ten, and, eventually, she might put two and two together. Get me?"

Ten got him. He nodded, his mind working.

"So, she better be quieted."

Ten nodded. "I'll take care of her, but one thing at a time, Comer. This job tonight first. Then her."

"Good enough."

"That all?"

"Isn't that enough?"

With a curt nod, Ten left. Comer slumped back in his chair, staring at the door. Ten was a killer with a reputation throughout that part of the west. He'd been with the Hardin gang, and the James boys. He had also done plenty on his own. It was rumored he had killed twenty men in face-to-face combat. No telling how many more he'd shot in the back. Comer had no doubt his first lieutenant had done just that. Ten was a practical killer. If necessary, he'd face a blazing revolver, but he'd as soon get the job done safely. There was nothing safer than a shot to the back.

Slick Comer didn't like Ten. He was a rattlesnake without rattles. He'd strike with silent deadliness. Slick also realized that his right-hand man was using him. Ten wanted the gang for his own, and he had a way of taking over in bits and pieces; as soon as the gunman felt confident he could handle a gang this size, he'd make his move.

Sooner or later, he and Ten would have a showdown. He was no match for such a killer, and he knew that as well. Ten would have to be taken out by somebody just as deadly.

The man who had just destroyed the GF brand smiled with satisfaction. He had that somebody. Just where he was right then, he didn't know, but he was on the way. He was the best; his reputation ranked high among hired killers. Comer, when the time was right, would set the pair against each other, Ten against a man called Stace.

Chapter Three

The gang met at twilight in Smith's Arroyo. They were a silent bunch of thirty hand-picked men. Slick Comer, leader of the entire enterprise, left the enlisting of gang members to his lieutenants. He trusted them to do this, because they knew the best type of man for rustling. Comer knew his chiefs, of course, and a few of the gang members, because of repeat performances, but the rank and file he did not know, nor did he wish to. There was no danger of the members talking too much in the aftermath of such raids. Ten handled the blabber mouths, and they knew it. Each member was well paid for his part, so silence, insofar as they were concerned, was both golden and life prolonging.

The darkening sky was chilly, but the men were prepared; they wore mackinaws and heavy jeans. They were also well-armed. Each was expected to furnish his own weapons.

Though the men had all been outlaws for many years, they were tense now. This would be the biggest job they'd ever taken on for many of them. Their horses felt the tension and were, themselves, skittish.

"Let's get on with it," Comer hissed to Ten. "We got to go forty miles to the EW herd, and we want to get there by midnight."

Rounding up the stolen cattle at that time would allow them to herd the animals to their special hideout for changing the brands. Everything was timework, and all there acknowledged it was Slick Comer's watch they would use.

Ten raised his hand. "No talking," he ordered. "We ride until we get the job done. No man turns back now." He touched his S&W. "Turn back, and I'll turn you under."

He laughed a silent laugh, but nobody joined him.

They had all seen Ten in action, and even the most hardened men, including Sierra and Jord, shuddered at the memory. Ten loved to kill. His face, taut and haunting, his eyes ablaze with blood lust, must have been a sight for those about to die.

They rode. The gang fanned out in a loose semi-circle at times, and at times rode single file. Their movements depended on the topography. They were single file when they stumbled onto Ruffy, the EW scout. He was at the point of turning back to the herd when he heard the gang approaching. He had been thinking about having a good time in Abilene. He knew a girl in one of the dance halls who favored him. He was also thinking about having a meal that hadn't been cooked in a Dutch oven for a change. Prune was a great camp cook, but restaurant feed was a treat.

Ruffy rode up to the men. He was curious.

"What's going on, fellas?" he asked. "Got a herd someplace out here?"

Ten stopped. "Where you from?" he asked pleasantly.

"Down south of here."

"EW?"

"Yeah."

"How far back?"

"About five miles."

Ten slipped his pistol out, said, "Thanks," and then shot Ruffy between the eyes.

The cowboy fell back off his saddle, and hit

the ground dead. His horse reared and galloped off.

"Get him," snapped Ten.

A couple of men rode down the nervous animal.

"You fool!" Slick was mad. "That shot could be heard for miles."

"We got five to go, according to him," he nodded at Ruffy's body, "pistol can't be heard that far, Slick. And knifing the man would have been too messy." He looked at his boss hard. "Any more objections?"

"Let's get on with it," Slick growled.

The gang moved ahead. The men rode in a kind of stupefied silence. They had all killed, but none so causally as this.

Leaving Ruffy sprawled in a bloody pool, the rustlers pushed on. At midnight, they slowed to a walk, stopping occasionally to listen.

During one of the pauses, Ten raised his hand. A faint sound reached their ears, a sound soft as cotton and keen as a knife blade.

Ten nodded. "That's cattle. Get ready."

The men knotted up under the sub-leaders.

"You fellers know what to do, and where we're goin'. Let's get this over with," Sierra said.

He glanced distastefully toward Ten, who sat in his saddle as straight as a ramrod. Ten then raised his hand again. "When I drop my hand, get to it. Don't let anybody see your face, kill as many men as you can, and get the cattle moving fast. Everything depends on speed."

Ten fired the first shot, and the luckless Jack fell.

The cattle were off and running, and the gang separated, each segment taking a proper place in and around the excited herd. EW cowboys dashed into the frantic scene, and shots were exchanged in great volleys.

In the dark confusion, Ten aimed at Slick Comer, but missed, and the opportunity vanished. The gunman cursed his luck, because it would have been a good time to get rid of their leader. Who would know who shot him with all that lead flying around?

But Ten wasn't one to dwell over missed opportunities. They usually came again—he was quite sure this one would.

He laughed his noiseless laugh and went to work, his pistol blazing.

Chapter Four

When Brad Tucker felt the bullet hit his shoulder, he knew this was a deadly game. Most rustlers would kill, but only if they had to. If confronted, they would shoot. They wanted cattle quickly, and without fuss from their guardians. Get in and get out, was the byword.

When they shot with purpose, and his shoulder wound was a shot that had missed his heart, the game was winner take all. These people had come not just after a few cows, but the entire herd. Just as the GF cattle had disappeared a month back. The word was out about this bold, deadly act. No man had been left alive.

He didn't shoot wildly. The racing shadows could be his own men. He raced toward the darker, scattered clumps, for they would not be his crew. Men at the chuckwagon had mounted at the first sound of gunfire. Even the cook, Prune, was on his horse. No man stood idle when trouble struck.

Stace and Red rushed up. "We're outnumbered!" shouted Stace. "Must be at least twenty of 'em!"

"Do what you can!"

Brad turned to Red. "You lay low, hear me?"

But the boy was having none of that. He charged off firing his .45 in the air, trying to divert cattle from what was fast becoming a stampede.

Shots and shouts split the air, the cattle bellowed and leaped ahead. Brad spied a group of men to the rear and drove Smoky toward them. They would be the crooks. As he rode, he let loose with his pistol, in an effort to hit one of the shadows. One let out a shriek Brad could hear even above the din, and he grinned. The figure slid off his horse. How many to go?

Out of the night he came face to face with a grim rider with sallow cheeks, and a blazing pistol. He was grinning horribly, as if he were enjoying every minute of the slaughter. Brad fired at him and was fired upon. Brad heard the lead whisper past his cheek, then the figure disappeared, caught up in the river of cattle.

The next instant, another man rode into view, his hat tilted back and his hair slicked back. The man fired, and again Brad fired back, but there was no satisfying screech. As had the first, the second man disappeared.

The boss of the EW herd took a moment to glance around. The shots were fewer now, and he saw less of what he figured were EW riders. He called for Stace and Red. No answer. The cattle were well on the move; the rustlers knew exactly what they were doing. Brad was shaken with a dreadful fear. None of the GF men had been left alive. Would this be another GF?

He rode along with the cattle to one side. Where were his men? His wound was beginning to take charge, and he felt a faintness. He circled back toward the chuckwagon. The fire was still burning with ironic faithfulness, but there were no cowhands in sight. The place mocked him with its emptiness.

The last of the cattle were passing now. A clump of four or five figures were behind, urging them on. Brad spurred Smoky after them, reloading his pistol as he rode. He yelled at them and fired when his weapon was ready. Once again, a figure lurched in the saddle and then toppled to the ground.

There was an immediate return of shots, a

regular hail of hot lead swept around Brad, but he charged on. There was no fear in him, no reticence, no second thoughts, no holding back. The heat of battle had taken over; he had no feelings at all, but only an idea: if his men had been killed then he, too, would be killed, but he'd take as many gunmen as he could with him.

The group was firing at him, and Brad saw others returning from the head of the herd. Fire bloomed from their pistols as well. Brad knew he couldn't last. It was inevitable that one of the bullets would find him. If he felt any emotion, had any thought, it was for Smoky. He hoped the big gelding wouldn't get hit.

And then it happened. A slug caught him in the chest, and flung him back in the saddle. Another caught him in the other shoulder, and threw him to the ground. When he hit, he landed on his left forearm. There was a snap, inaudible during the huge commotion, and then Brad was still.

When Brad came to, he was in a wide bed. That was the first thing he noticed. The second thing he knew as his senses cleared, was that the room was yellow. It was a bright, canary yellow. There were two corner windows in the room, and they were both open. A cross breeze waved gauzy curtains gently, creating a soundless dance.

"How are you?"

The voice was feminine and light, but firm.

Brad craned his neck around in an effort to see, but he was very weak, and gave up. He rolled his eyes sideways instead, and even that was an effort. A girl bent over him. Her dark eyes were full of concern and sympathy.

"Where am I?" he managed in a voice he scarcely recognized.

"The Abilene Hotel," was the quiet reply. Even in that critical moment of voice introduction, Brad liked the sound. It was very clear. He understood the words perfectly in his foggy world.

"Why am I here?"

"You were shot in three places, and your arm is broken. The doctor put you here, because there was no place else to take you."

The scene was returning to Brad slowly. He opened his mouth to ask about his men and the cattle when weakness overtook his words. He mumbled, then slipped into a deep sleep.

When he came to again, a lamp burned on a table across the room. The windows were still open, but night had fallen. The yellow walls were soft in the light. Brad was seized by a tremendous thirst.

"Water," he whispered through dry lips.

The girl was at his side at once. She lifted his head gently, and held a glass to his lips. Brad sipped. When he was finished, she lay his head back on the pillow and placed the glass on a stand near him.

"If you're thirsty while I'm gone," she said, "you can help yourself. I think you're strong enough."

Brad suddenly remembered what had taken place. He recalled the midnight riders and that there was a large gang of them. He recalled the fight and remembered yelling out for Stace and Red. He felt again the slap of bullets in his chest and shoulder.

"What happened to—ah, the cattle?" he asked. Then, very carefully, slowly, because he didn't want to know what he expected was the answer. "What about my men?"

The girl's face was composed and sad.

"Your cattle, except for about two hundred, are gone."

She had long, brown hair that fell over her shoulders like a silky shawl. She brushed it back.

"So are most of your men." She hesitated. "They are gone."

Brad stared at the girl. He was hearing what he didn't want to hear.

"What do you mean by 'gone'?"

"I think you know, Brad. I think you know what I mean."

She touched him on his hand.

"Three men are still with you."

"Three?" Brad heard himself repeating her words and felt stupid, but he could think of nothing else to say through his shock. "Three? All the rest are dead? How?"

"Shot, or crushed by the cattle when they stampeded."

"My God," groaned the injured man. "Oh, my heavens," and he buried his face in his hands.

The girl touched his hand once again. "Do you," her voice was controlled and gentle, "want to see the three?"

Brad nodded. He felt anger, pity, and tears all welling up at the same time.

The girl left for a few minutes to return with Stace and Red. Their faces were lined with the strain of what they'd been through. Young Red's eyes were rimmed with tear stains. Long Jim and Blacky had teased him as a "green kid," while at the same time showing him how to rope, and take care of cattle sores; Scarecrow and Jack, along with Ruffy, had showed him how to ride trail, what to do when a stray insisted on remaining stray, and free; Ruffy had even given him a kerchief to cover his mouth with when trail dust got thick.

"We thought you was a goner," said Stace, taking his boss's hand.

"You was pretty well shot up," agreed Red.

"All the men dead?" Brad forced himself to ask that terrible question. He knew he could trust the girl's knowledge, but he wanted Stace to say it for some reason.

"All except Prune, though he got himself scratched by a slug."

"What about Ruffy?"

"We never found him," said the boy. He was pale. This was a facet about cowboying he hadn't dreamed of. He'd heard of rustlers. Anybody who lived in the west heard about them, and what happened to them if they were caught. Hung until dead—on the spot, no trial.

"We tried tracking the herd," said Stace, "but no chance."

"Too many herds coming this way," said the girl. "There's no telling by the tracks which way yours went."

"After four days, and five more herds coming into Abilene, we don't have a chance tracking down ours."

Those particular words riveted Brad's attention.

"You say four days. How long I been here?"

"Well, it took a day to get you to town, and you been in bed three days since."

"Three days in this room?"

"Yep!"

Brad felt his face heat up. His entire body heated up. He was embarrassed to the core.

He glanced shyly at the girl. "I mean, Miss, surely there was a nurse, or somebody like that taking care of me."

"No. I was the one."

Brad nearly lost his tongue. "You took care of me for everything?"

"Don't be embarrassed. I did a lot of nursing when I was on trail drives with the GF."

Brad caught the brand. "You mean, ah, that is—well, the GF?"

He paused not sure how to go on, or if he should.

"Yes, that GF, Brad." The girl's voice turned hard and bitter. "That was my daddy's outfit. His cattle were stolen just like yours, only he didn't get off like you did. He was killed."

Brad didn't know what to say, but for the first time, he noticed grief in the girl's eyes.

"I'm so sorry," he muttered.

The girl smiled sadly. "Thanks. Thank you."

"No witnesses," growled Stace. "Listen, I been on the outside of the law, but I ain't never seen anything like this. They, whoever they are, aimed to wipe us all out like bugs."

"How did you manage to escape?"

"We hid in the dust, and weren't seen is all. Just plain luck. They didn't look long. They figure they got us all."

"That's it!" The girl's voice lost its melody. "Your EW outfit got it just like we did, except four of you got away." She focused on Brad. "Did you see anybody you'd recognize now?"

He explained the two men, who came out of the dark shooting.

She stiffened. "I'll bet my life those two are Slick Comer and Ten. They do business here in town. But it'd be hard to prove."

"Why's that?"

"They'd have a dozen witnessses to prove they were someplace else. Probably members of the gang. I've had my eye on them."

"Why are you here?" Brad asked. "And not back at your ranch?"

"I was at the ranch when word came what happened. I came here to—bury my father, and what was left of the boys killed with him."

She paused, struggling with tears, then went on. "There was no use staying at the ranch. There are people to take care of it. Like I say, I want to find out who did this terrible thing. I won't rest until I know. Not ever."

Brad spoke gently. "How come you're nursing me?"

"Because I was just living, getting by day by day, watching for somebody to make a mistake. The doctor can't be here all the time. He's got other patients, so I volunteered." She gave him a straight look. "I felt close to you, because I know what you will have to go through to come to grips with this. I thought we'd work together to solve these horrible crimes."

In answer to Brad's questioning eyes, she added, "I'm Gail Fanchy. George Fanchy's daughter."

Brad had suspected something of the sort.

"I am so sorry," he told her, "about that tragedy. So, sorry!" He held her hand. "We'll get them, I promise."

The girl leaned toward him, but caught herself.

"We'll work together," she said. "I must find the killers who murdered my father and the crew—all of them were friends of mine."

"And my crew the same," said Brad. "The same." He turned to Red. "Sorry, I got you into this, son."

The boy glanced at Stace. "He's showing me how to use my pistol right."

"Just be careful. This isn't a child's game."

Red stiffened. "I ain't a child, boss, not now."

Brad nodded. "Of course not." To Stace. "Has Ed Warshal been notified?"

"Sent him a wire right off."

"How about Smokey, my good partner?"

"He's in the barn, ready to go again."

The wounded man's eyes drooped. He felt like he could sleep forever. Whatever stuff the doctor had given him to ease the pain was working overtime.

All was done that could be done, it seemed to him.

"He was lucky to have you here," Stace said to Gail.

"I was glad to help." She eyed Stace's low-slung .45's. "Will you help find these awful people?"

Stace nodded. "You can count on it one hundred percent."

"Me, too," added Red.

"Keep an eye on Comer and Ten," the girl advised.

"Ten?" Stace frowned. "He's here?"

"You know him?"

"By reputation only. He's a bad one."

"I knew it!" The girl was pleased that her suspicions were validated. "We'll work together on this?"

"Along with him." Stace nodded at the now sleeping Brad Tucker. "He's the boss. I take orders from him, but," he shrugged, "in the meantime, while he gets better, it won't hurt if me and Red have a look around."

They left the girl. Once in the street, Stace told the boy to get the cook, Prune, and have something to eat. He'd connect with them both later.

"We got more practicing to do with my shooting," Red reminded him.

"Later." Then Stace added words that puzzled him. "But you don't want to get too good at it."

With that he was off, and the boy returned to their hotel to find the cook. The cook was gone. He was, the clerk told him, gone forever, headed for San Francisco to join a merchant ship bound for China, or someplace far off where it was safer.

Stace went to the marshal's office first. A man by the name of Tom Smith had been given the position by the people of Abilene. Stace had contacted the lawman first thing after seeing his boss was in the care of a doctor.

"Anything, Marshal?"

Tom Smith, a man who had plenty of experience in western law keeping, shook his head.

"Nothing. No clues. We got men out looking. We even sent for Pinkerton detectives.

This has happened four times in two years, and it has got to be stopped."

"The Pinkertons here yet?"

"Not enough time—still, they might be. They don't exactly shout out their whereabouts."

The marshal knew about Stace. He knew the man he was talking to was a gunhand, that he'd served time in a Texas jail and paid his debt to society. What he didn't know was whether the man had really reformed. Gunsels sometimes liked their work too much. It looked good for Stace that he was doing legitmate work as a trail hand on a long trip. It showed determination. But Tom Smith meant to keep his eye on the man anyway.

On leaving the marshal's office, Stace headed for the upstairs office in the Alamo, where Slick Comer resided. Half an hour later, he emerged. There were new shadows in his eyes.

Back in the room where Brad Tucker slept, Gail Fanchy sat quietly. She was deeply saddened by her father's violent end. She was also angered that the murder had been committed for money. There was nothing constructive in murder and rustling for the money in it. Nothing. It was an exercise in futility. She hated what had happened, and was determined to find the men who had planned and carried out such cruelty.

She was sure Slick Comer and the gaunt, dark man called Ten were at the bottom of it. She had no proof, but she sensed she was right—woman's intuition perhaps? Why not! It was as good a reason as any. Besides, that was all she had to go on. That, and the descriptions Brad had given her of the pair at the fight.

She glanced at the sleeping man whom she had nursed for the past three days. He was young, and, while asleep, seemed so innocent and untroubled. Could he help her enough? Would he? And what was Stace to him? There was something about Stace that bothered her. He walked softly, almost catlike, on the balls of his feet. He walked like a man who had a reason for walking softly. He was direct in his manner, and yet there was also something in his manner that was hidden.

The girl shook her mind free of her suspicions and felt Brad's forehead. He wasn't so feverish now. The doctor's medicines were helping. Brad's chest wound had been the worst. The slug hadn't torn anything vital, but went deep, and the doctor had to dig to get it out.

The wounded man would be up and around in a few weeks. And then? Would they start searching for the killers of her father then?

Tears came to her eyes, and as she sat in her chair, faithful to her post, she wept.

Chapter Five

Ed Warshal arrived a week after he received word. He'd ridden hard over a rough, long trail, and was tired. The first thing he did, though, was stride to Brad Tucker's sick room. Warshal, a man of about fifty, white-haired, strong-jawed, blue-eyed, was a man of contradictions. Friends knew him in two lights: a pussycat on the one hand, but a man of iron on the other.

He bounded across the room and grabbed Brad's hand.

"Great Scott, boy!" he thundered, "what a terrible thing!"

"It wasn't good," Brad admitted, who by then was able to sit in bed. He could even go to the john by himself, which was a relief. He took Warshal's hand, which was so large it covered his own considerable appendage like a blanket.

"I hear all the boys were killed! Unbelievable! Terrible! Terrible!" A pause, then quietly, "Any of the bodies ever found?"

Brad told about how Red, Stace, Prune, and himself were the only survivors. "But," he continued, "we found all the bodies. They were badly cut up by stampeding cattle, and they'd all been shot. But we didn't find Ruffy, who had been scouting."

"Anybody working on this? Got the law involved?"

"Tom Smith, the marshal, has had men out to the site all week. But there's been five herds come in since we got shot up, and there isn't much to go on. No tracks that make any sense."

Gail had been out of the room and returned at this moment. Brad introduced her, and told him how she was involved.

"So," the pussycat in Ed Warshal came to the fore, "you lost your good Daddy, eh?" He nodded. "Yes, I heard about that tragedy. Word gets around." He took her in his great arms as he'd known her all his life, and hugged her to him. "What a loss, girl, what a loss."

And Gail, though she'd scarely had time for more than a 'hello,' allowed herself to be hugged. It felt good, and she needed to be held close. A complete stranger was giving her more comfort by a simple act of kindness than she'd received since leaving the GF ranch.

Warshal released her gently. "I take it, little lady, you want those killers brought to justice?"

"I want them, Mr. Warshal. Oh, how I want them."

The boss of the EW nodded. "Yes, we all do. We'll work as a team, your GF, and my EW." He turned to Brad. "How soon you going to be out of here, lad?"

"Another week, Ed."

"More like three," interrupted Gail.

Warshal grinned. "Only thing good come out of this—she's been your nurse, son?"

Brad nodded.

"Only good thing," said Ed Warshal with another smile. To Brad, "I'm putting money in the bank for expenses. You can draw on it as needed. Get busy solving this, as soon as," he glanced at Gail, "your nurse says it's all right. I can't stay. I've got half a dozen other ranches that need my attention. You work with Gail here, and whatever men she can get from her home ranch. You say the law hasn't got anything yet?"

"No, but Tom Smith is a good man. He'll dig."

"We're all going to have to dig, and maybe deep. These raids have been planned by clever men. Any suspects at all?"

Brad told him about Comer and Ten.

"Work from them, then. And, how about Stace?"

"Stace?" Brad was startled.

"I've heard about him, Brad. He was a bad one once. Kind of surprised you hired him."

Brad flushed. "I'll vouch for him, Ed. He's all right."

"Your judgement has always been good, that's why you're trail boss. But it's hard for a gun to clean itself. Now, now!" He raised his hand, as Brad's discomfort increased. "I don't mean to set friend against friend, Brad, but you have to remember I've had a considerable loss in cattle and good men. The cattle can be replaced. The men can't, and I want them avenged. I have to cover all possibilities, do you understand?"

"Yes, I get it, Ed."

"All right, then. Stace is your man and your reponsibility; I got to have that understanding." That was Ed Warshal the iron man. "Now, I got to get me a bath and a barber shave. I smell awful after all that time on the trail. Besides," and the pussycat appeared, "I want to take your lady to dinner." He turned to Gail. "May I?"

She was surprised, but accepted graciously. She'd been dining alone. It would be nice to have company.

My lady, thought Brad. *My* lady?

The following days passed like eternal hell for him. He chafed at his wounds, tested himself prematurely, wanting the healing to hurry and do its job. A great mystery waited for him. Who had done this terrible thing? It was a mystery which had to be solved, and would be solved if it took him the rest of his life.

"Gail," he groaned, "why don't we heal faster?"

The girl smiled, one of the few she had committed to since her father's death.

"You're impatient as a child," she chided, "you can't hurry mother nature."

"Huh," grunted a dissatisfied trail boss. "I'd like to kick old mama nature you know where, and get her moving."

After a few days, Ed Warshal left.

"You're in complete charge," he reaffirmed with Brad. "Oh, I've talked to your man, Stace. He's polite, but there's something hidden. Be careful."

"You remember when you took me in, and

made me into something, Ed? Remember what you said when I thanked you for giving me a chance? You said, 'Pass it on.' Well, I'm doing that with Stace."

The owner of the EW ranch nodded. "Yes, and you're right. Still . . ." He turned to Gail, and hugged her.

"I'm going to miss those hugs," she admitted.

With a glint in his eye, Ed Warshal said, "You're going to have to take over on these hugs, Brad."

Caught off guard, Brad turned red, and stammered what he thought was a good attempt to maintain composure. "Sure . . . ah . . . of course."

Even Gail laughed at that. "Well," she teased, "you don't have to be so excited about it."

But, Brad noticed, there was a look in her eyes that set the teasing aside. He was sharp enough to notice it.

When Warshal spoke again, his voice was deadly serious.

"Brad, you have Stace, Gail, and Red working on this matter. The marshal is in on it with a posse, but, sometimes, you have to take matters in your own hands. I'm not advocating you go against the authorities; work with them, but you also have to shape up what could be called Tucker's law. You have do a lot for yourself."

Brad understood. Tucker's law! He hadn't put it in quite that grandiose a phrase, but he understood his employer. The marshal was a good man, and would do all he could. Still, there was nothing like the personal touch. He nodded.

"Good."

His employer extended one of those hams he called hands, and enclosed Brad's.

"I'll be waiting to hear. Act fast, don't let the shadows grow, and don't let any who doesn't have to know in on it."

Alone with Gail, Brad felt extremely awkward. He didn't know what to say, and limped painfully to the window, where he gazed silently into the street.

"You two are close," the girl said, breaking the ice.

"He's like a father. Listen, about that hugging, and all . . ."

Her response surprised him. "Well, Brad Tucker, I don't think you should carry on about it."

"What?"

"Am I that bad?"

"Well, no, of course not. I don't mind you at all."

With irony, "Well, thanks for not minding me at all."

Brad spoke earnestly, too earnestly sometimes.

"I'd have died without you Miss Fanchy . . ."

"Gail."

"Miss Gail, ah, Gail I mean. You have been a tremendous help, you and the poison the doctor has been feeding me."

"I'm glad you are happy, Mr. Tucker."

"Brad, please." He paused. "Am I doing something wrong here?"

Gail, not knowing quite why she'd been so wayward with her attitude, said, "No, no, Brad. I think I'm just tired is all." She looked at him. "So what is the next step?"

Brad felt relief at the girl's change in attitude—though, actually, he didn't know quite why he should.

"Look," he said, "the main thing holding me up is my arm. It's still in a sling, but the shoulders and chest are doing all right. I think I'm strong enough to ride, and I need to get out of this yellow room. I see yellow in my dreams. So, let's ride!"

"Where to?"

"Let's go back to where the raid on my herd took place. Let's follow the trails straight from Abilene, as much as we can." He looked at her. "Are you ready for some painful reminders?"

She nodded, though slowly. "Yes, we have

to do that. We'll pass the place where we think my father's cattle were stolen. We can't be sure, because there were no survivors, but it's about where he'd have been." She paused, then added softly, "He would want that."

"We'll gather up Stace and Red. Four pairs of eyes are better than two."

"Why doesn't Mr. Warshal like Stace?"

"You understood that?"

"He was cold to him most of the time. There must be a reason."

Brad pulled no punches.

"Stace served time in jail for murder. He was able, in time, to prove self-defense, but he does have a reputation."

"As a what, a gunman?"

"Something like that."

"But you trust him?"

He told her about the five-to-one fight where he'd met Stace.

"Ed has said my instincts are pretty good about men, so, yes, I trust him."

"Time will tell."

"We better make plans."

"What about Comer and Ten? I'm sure those two are men of the worst kind, but there's no proof, yet."

"You can bet we'll get to them, but one thing at a time."

They left early the next morning. Brad rode Smoky, and managed well enough with his one hand. Brad spoke to the horse, "Good boy, good boy. I'm so glad you weren't hurt, my friend." He gave the animal an affectionate pat on the arched neck. "You and I, you and I, Smoky."

The horse snorted, as he always did when Brad spoke in that particular private voice.

Brad laughed. It was good to hear his friend agreeing.

Stace, riding a bit ahead of the others, grinned back at them.

"Nice to have a horse who understands us." He repeated Brad's thoughts, "Good to have four pair of human eyes on the scene, and those of a talking horse."

It was obvious that the boy, Red, was stricken with Stace. He hung on the man's words. Apparently, everything that Stace said was whole wisdom to him. He and Stace had spent a lot of time together since the tragedy. He was learning first-class marksmanship. Brad noticed the closeness of the two and wondered at Ed Warshal's concern over the ex-gunman. Would he influence the boy too much? He had to shrug off that concern. Right now, he wanted to find killers, rustlers, tough, bad hombres. He reckoned that Stace and Red would have to manage their own lives without his interference. But he couldn't help paying closer attention to Stace. Had he really given up gunplay? There was no harm in Stace showing Red how to shoot. Was there?

The foursome traced the ground thoroughly, from where the chuckwagon had been as far as the herd's tracks could be clearly seen. There was debris, a broken pistol, a trampled hat, a torn red kerchief.

It was Gail who located Ruffy. He was lying on his side, swollen from the heat, his body disintegrating. Mice and other carnivores had eaten the flesh. It was a terrible sight to see.

"Great heavens," she murmured, suddenly sick.

So were the others. The sight, though horrific, couldn't compare to the stench.

Brad noted the hole in Ruffy's foreheard, and the mystery of how he had died was suddenly clear.

"Shot in cold blood," he muttered.

Then he saw a glistening object on the ground. It was a .44 caliber case. Most men carried .45's, but not all. Forty-fours were legitimate in the country. As a clue to the death of Ruffy, it wasn't much.

"Whoever shot Ruffy," observed Brad, "reloaded. Mostly likely he was expecting a lot of use, and wanted a full cylinder."

"Most gunfighters I know," added Stace, "would do that. They'd reload right off."

"You mean that fellow, Ten, is a gunman?"

"From what I've seen of him in the last month, it's possible," Gail put in. "He had an arrogant air about him. And," she added to that, "if that was Ten you saw when your herd was rustled, it seems to me two and two add up to one."

Stace nodded. "Yes, I know about him. He has a reputation. You want me to learn more about him?"

"Do you know the right places to investigate?"

"Brad, I've been in the business a long time."

Brad nodded. Did Stace know more about Ten than he was saying? Would he challenge Ten? That would be a shortcut, by getting rid of an enemy, but if Stace was successful in a gunfight, he would be outside the law again. Or he could be killed, if the man, Ten, was as good as he was supposed to be.

"You stay clear, Stace. I'll handle it."

"We're all in this, boss."

"I know, and before it's over, we'll be in deeper than we want. For now, let me do the talking."

Stace nodded. Orders were orders, but Brad had a hunch Stace would act on his own if he saw the need.

They buried Ruffy and returned to town. Brad went to the marshal's office to report the death.

Tom Smith evaluated the news carefully. He never took a death offhand.

Finally, he said, "A connection, you suppose, with the EW rustling?"

"And this was used." Brad showed the lawman the .44 shell.

Smith examined it. "Yeah, .44. Not too scarce around here, but at least we know what the weapon probably was."

"What do you think about Slick Comer and Ten?"

"Been keeping an eye on Ten in particular. I know his reputation."

"And?"

"Ten arrived two, three years back, when Comer was your average cattle buyer. After Ten arrived, Comer seems to have had a lot of cattle himself. He's got pretty fat."

"He hasn't got a ranch, Marshal. So he hasn't got any homegrown stock."

"I know, but a lot of these buyers try to beat each other to the punch and go downtrail to meet the herds. I figure that's what Comer is doing."

"Yeah, but there's been four big herds rustled in the past three years."

"Sure, but I can't prove anything. No proof that those two citizens were involved. You can't hang 'em on suspicion, and," he added quickly, seeing the question rise in Brad's eyes, "I haven't got the manpower to play detective. Abilene, my friend, is enough for me."

"Suppose I get proof."

"You do that, and I'll lock 'em up. Oh, by the way . . ."

"Yes?"

"That man of yours, Stace. He's got a record, you know."

"I know. But he's kicked the habit."

The marshal's chuckle was really amused. "You think that, and I'll sell you the ocean. Never trust a 'reformed' gunman. Man, he could be in with Comer and Ten."

"I'll take him at his word, and he's good on the trail."

"Sure, looking over your herd, maybe? Front man for Comer?"

Brad left the marshal's office partly angry. Why was everybody on Stace? The man had done nothing against the law as long as he'd known him. Why the hits? He knew the answer to that even as he asked the question. Once and ex-con, always an ex-con. Once a gunman, always a gunman. Stace would always come under suspicion. He'd been a bad one in the past. People like Smith, and even Warshal, who tried to understand the man, wouldn't really trust him.

He returned to the hotel. Gail's room was not far from his, and he decided to see if she was in. He knocked on the door when, to his surprise, he heard boots thumping inside. There was a confusion of sounds, and among them came Gail's voice, weak and shaky, "Help! Help me!"

Brad reacted at once. He tried the door. Locked. Without hesitation, he lifted a booted foot and smashed it open. Gail, crumpled and gasping for breath, lay on the bed. A window was open, and Brad dashed over to it, but saw nothing. Whoever had caused the trouble was gone.

He whirled to Gail. She sat up, rubbing her neck where two red welts were rising. He sat next to her, caught her in his arms, and held her close.

"What's going on?"

"There were two men. They were waiting when I came into the room."

"What . . . ?" Brad hesitated. "Did . . . ?"

Gail guessed the question.

"No," she shivered, "they did nothing like that. I think they wanted to kill me, but I fought, and you came," she rubbed the welts on her neck, "just in time, Brad, just in time, I was beginning to black out."

"Did you get a good look at them?"

"One had light, blond hair, the other a deep scar down his cheek, and a black, curved down mustache." She shrank into Brad's arms. "He said terrible things to me. I've never heard such language."

Brad Tucker felt a rage growing in him, a molten, white hot rage. He also felt a tremendous protectiveness toward the girl. He hugged her closely, and she responded with tears.

"They were awful, Brad."

And he made up his mind; those were two men who would, eventually, wish they'd never been born.

Chapter Six

Brad remained with Gail for the rest of the day. They reported the incident, and near tragedy, to Marshal Smith. He was as angered as Tucker. Two deputies were dispatched throughout the town in search of a man with blond hair and another with a handlebar mustache and a facial scar.

"Cattle drives are good for this town," Smith grumbled. "Without them, there wouldn't be much, but they bring in all kinds of rot." He took Gail's hand. "Sorry this happened in my town, Missy."

"Why," Gail was puzzled, "were they so intent on taking my life?"

Brad was suddenly tense. "You've been

looking into your father's death. Maybe somebody thinks you are getting too close for comfort."

Gail gave him a nod of agreement. "But I don't know anything, just suspicions are all."

"Maybe," added the marshal, "that's enough. Suspicions can open doors. I'm putting a guard in your hall tonight."

But Gail declined the guard. "I don't think they'll dare come back now." She glanced at Brad. "Especially when they know somebody is after them."

She sounded much more confident than she felt but saw no reason to further the incident. Brad's room was only a door or two from hers, anyway. She'd be all right.

Later, when she bid Brad goodnight, she clung to him for a moment. "Thanks, my friend. Thank you so much."

He nodded. "I'll sleep with both eyes open. Yell if you need help."

In spite of her brave words, once she was in the privacy of her room, and alone with her thoughts, she found she was in shock. She'd lived all her life on the western frontier, and never, not ever, been even remotely afraid for her life or body. Her ranch was in the south of Kansas, near the town of Lisbon, as isolated as a spread could be, but she had never known fear.

Gail knew ranchers and cowboys well. As soon as she was able to ride a horse well enough, her father took her on branding missions. She learned the rough ways of the frontier early on.

When she was fourteen, she went on her first trail drive, a long haul to California. She survived such dangers as snakes, scorpions, flooding rivers, dangerous passes through the Sierra Nevada mountains, and the inconveniences of camp life for women.

She had also shared in the camaradie of that journey, and many others following. The men gathered around the fire at night and sang the old songs, such as "A Cowboy's Dream," to the tune of "My Bonnie Lies Over The Ocean," or "The Kansas Line," a favorite song full of homesickness, and longing for a true female friend.

While she was still inexperienced, she took the good-natured hazing of the crew on the trail. They sent her from the point of the herd, the leading edge, back to the drag, the very rear, where dust from a thousand hoofs billowed. They sent her to camp for "hock grease" for the foot weary cattle. There was no such thing as hock grease, but the trick brought delight to the crew. They warned her about the Mountain Ghost, when she took her turn at night hawking, and made spooky noises in the dark to frighten her.

After awhile her reputation as a good hand with horses grew. The men respected her ability. They were among the best riders in the world, and knew a good one they they saw her. She was considered high on the list. Theirs was a respect she treasured.

Never once, not once, in all the time she had been with them was there an attempt at anything offensive. They even tried to guard their language, which was not Sunday school recommended. The work being what it was, difficult, and at times dangerous, they sometimes forgot, but they tried. They treated her in most respects as one of their own. When she was working she took orders not from her father, but from the foreman, or trail boss, and followed those orders as would any man.

What was more, she grew to respect the men she worked with. Badly educated, hard drinkers when on a spree, chasers of 'tainted women,' they were also honest, and proud of their abilities. They were quick tempered and got into fights, but were loyal to their kind, to their boss. Their creed was "A good day's work for a good day's pay." They rode into danger without complaint, taking it all in as part of the job.

If a rambunctious young cowboy sometimes made calf eyes at her, she took it with good humor. If sometimes after a month on the trail, an older hand was caught glancing at her speculatively, he blushed to the roots of his hair.

Gail knew instinctively about those feelings. She realized that men were different than women. She'd gone to dances in Lisbon, and had seen other girls disappear from the floor with their partners. They might be gone for ten minutes or an hour, and she didn't need to be told why. She knew enough.

It was rare she'd hear about rape, but it happened. The West was not populated solely by noble youth or men who blushed to the roots of their hair over an inadvertent glance. There was the other side, the perverts, the robber gangs, the Indian marauders, the Mexican rebels from south of the border, and the just plain bad ones. They were the collective group who plundered, killed, rustled, and raped. They were the ones who, if caught, were immediately hanged. There was no second chance, nor was any expected.

Gail's home life had been solid. Her mother had been a good homemaker, fashioning respectability out of a frontier wasteland. It was she who set a regular table and wouldn't allow the family to slip into sloppy eating habits. It was she who, along with Gail when the girl was old enough, kept the house clean, and it was she who kept decent clothing on the backs of the family. It was her mother, who told Gail to watch her heart. She did not tell her daughter about sex, because sex was never mentioned, but she advised Gail to have a good time within the limits of common sense, and to enjoy life, because, as she put it, "Life only comes around once, dear."

Gail's father, a hard worker, was a success in a tough, competitive business. He was rightfully proud of his accomplishments. He took pride in his home, a large, two-storied house of planed, seasoned lumber, a rarity in the region. He painted it white, another rarity. Nobody painted houses; they left the lumber to turn gray with age, and weather. George Fanchy reckoned a paint job would preserve the wood, aside from "prettying it up," and he was correct. The Fanchy place never wore the bored and weary look of so many other ranch houses. He and his wife shared a loving relationship, until her death from the flu.

The girl grew up respected and loved in a secure home. Her environment had been close and protected. Now, in Abilene, she was not so protected. She was a woman alone, except for Brad Tucker. For the first time, she faced life without her father and the crew of men whom she had looked on as part of the family. She had learned how much she could lose to seemingly senseless violence. Not all men respected her, not all were friends.

Ever since the death of her father, the mantra that had said harm not and you won't be harmed, had been ripped apart. Her ideals were shaken, and the promise that the world was good had collapsed. She had not been foolish; she had known there were bad things in the world—rustling, robberies, murder—but she never realized those bad things could happen to her. They happened in other homes, on other ranges. Now, her view had been changed by two nothings who called themselves men. They had breached the sanctity of her inner fortress. Two thugs had forced her into a retreat, two who had death, and possibly rape, on their minds. She would never, and she knew this with certainty, be the same again; she would never be so wholly at ease with the world again. A part of her had been slain by a pair of spiritless thugs.

Her mood, goaded by a sudden restlessness, and a growing anger, could lead to only one solution. She opened a saddle bag and withdrew a .45 Colt revolver. Her father had given it to her, and she now realized the gift had been for more than just practice. He knew about the dangers of the world, and he wanted her to be prepared.

Thank you, Dad, she thought to herself, *you are my protector even though you are no longer with me.*

She had worn the gun on the trail to help head the stock in the right direction, but she never wore it in town.

She was a good shot, because her father insisted that she learn.

"Never use a gun you can't use well," had been his advice.

She retrieved the cartridge belt and holster from the closet and strapped the assembly around her waist. She checked the pistol's cylinder, making sure it was filled, then sunk the weapon into the holster. The weight was comforting and felt protective.

She left the room, not exactly sure what she was going to do, or in which direction to go. The pair of would-be killers had probably left town by now—or had they? Such arrogance wasn't smart enough to know fear. She'd try the bars rather than wander the street. Bars were most likely her best chance.

Women such as Gail Fanchy didn't frequent bars. Dance hall girls worked the bars, and prostitutes used them as a headquarters.

Rarely did a woman of Gail's social standing enter them, especially alone.

She was self-conscious as she drew stares. She was well dressed in a long blue riding skirt, a white blouse, and a white, felt hat, with a wide brim, and flat crown. It was held in place by a braided leather thong. When she entered through the batwing doors, there were stares, then a polite, if startled, silence. Even the drunks paused in their blathering.

In each bar, she asked the same question of the bartender.

"Have you seen two men, one with a face scar, and handlebar mustache, and the other with blond hair?"

Her question brought soft, reserved answers. "Why, no, ma'am, hain't seen any like that aroun' yere."

Finally, though, she received a nod.

Gail's heart jumped. "Where?"

"It was four to five days ago, ma'am. They stopped by for a few minutes."

"But not today?"

"No. Is they somethin' wrong?"

Gail evaded the question. The matter was too complicated to go into. She was fully aware that to go into details about her life and death struggle would be too much for the men to absorb so quickly, but, her asking was deliberate. If word got out to the pair that she was looking for them by description, they might come to her to finish the job they started. Her descriptions could be deadly to them. She wanted that. If the huntress couldn't find the quarry, she could use bait to attract that quarry.

There were only a couple of bars left. Darkness had replaced the sun, and darkness was similarly crowding Gail's hopes. She still didn't know just what she was going to do if she confronted the two. She decided to play her cards as they were dealt. Haul them to the marshal? Challenge them to a gun battle? She was still angry enough to respond to any opening.

When she reached the Applejack, a bar famed in that part of the west for its various amusements, her caution took on an edge. The place was crowded. It would be easy for two thugs to melt away. Cowboys with three months' wages in their pockets were bellied up to the bar for refreshments, card games were in progress at round tables covered with green velvet cloth, and dance hall girls were raking the money in by charging for each dance. Advertising posters on the walls told of an acting troupe in town with a Shakespeare play, *Hamlet*. The Bard was popular with the rank and file. There were many rough and tumble cowpokes who knew about the unfortunate Dane.

What Gail found, though, was a surprise. Brad was leaning on the bar, smiling at her, though his eyes were serious.

"Have you had any luck?" he asked.

"Luck with what?" she hedged, though she wasn't quite sure he knew why she was there, wearing a .45.

"Don't make me spell it out, Gail."

She fingered the butt of her pistol. "They have it coming, Brad."

"And they'll get it, Gail. That kind always do, but not here and not now."

"Why not?"

"I think you already know why. Those two are long gone. Or, at least, well hidden. They don't dare show their faces."

"The cowards!" The girl's anger broke loose.

"Would you have shot them?" Brad was curious.

Gail shook her head. "I don't know. I just don't know, but maybe. I'd have to have seen the moves they made. I'd have done something!"

"Better let it go for now. Let's get some coffee and relax you a bit."

Gail was ready to cease the search. What would she have done? If she had killed them, what proof did she have that they'd attacked her? Could the marshal have held them on her say-so?

Suddenly, she was tired. Bone weary. The whole gigantic nightmare fell back on her, like a dark cloak. Her anger dissolved. As Brad had pointed out, someday, somewhere, those two would be dealt with. Life had a way of evening up scores. For now, all she could hope for was that the day would soon come.

She left the building, followed by Brad.

"How did you know?" she asked.

"Word gets around."

He didn't tell her the fear he really harbored. Somebody wanted her dead. So much so, that a rifle could be waiting in an alley. In the meantime, he'd stick close to Gail Fanchy. He admired her. Courage had prompted her to seek the killers of her father and his crew. She didn't cut and run. She was here, she was determined, she meant to find those responsible.

That was enough for Brad Tucker.

Chapter Seven

Marshal Tom Smith was a practical man. When he knew he couldn't handle a job alone, he sent for help. After he'd heard about the near rape and killing of Gail Fanchy, he realized there was more skullduggery underfoot than he could dig out. He handled outright crooks, the robbers, your everyday range rustlers, card sharks, and thugs with ease. He was a tough man, but when matters grew murky, when motives were twilight shadows, he knew where to go.

After the GF mass rustling job, and the killings, he'd wired the Pinkerton National Detective Agency in Chicago. Now after the EW repeat, plus the attempt on Gail's life, he sent another message, "Where in blazes is your help? Urgent! Urgent!"

In the Alamo Bar occupying the upstairs office, two men in business suits and Texas high-heeled boots were talking.

"Well," said one, "that sure misfired. Where are those two jackasses now, Comer?"

"I sent them to the hideout, Ten, with instructions to lay low." He shook his head. "I don't understand it. They've done jobs like that before; they're good men. That fellow, Brad Tucker, flushed them out."

"Couldn't they have finished him and the girl at the same time?"

"Wasn't their job to kill anybody else, Ten, so they beat it."

"So now what?" The gunman was tense. "Do you think the girl was scared enough to quit snooping?"

"No." Comer was thoughtful. "I hear she was looking for those two that attacked her. So we got to do it another way."

"We still kill her?"

"That's right."

"There's more behind this, isn't there?" Ten's eyes narrowed.

Comer nodded. "With her dead, her looking where she's not supposed to look will stop. But more than that, with her gone, the GF will be up for grabs. She's sole owner since her daddy died. I want that ranch."

"Tucker is backing her up."

"Then we'll have to get both of them."

"Like I say, should have been done before."

Comer shrugged. "But it wasn't. Got any ideas?"

"Ambush is the simplest." Ten smiled. "Very simple."

"Yes, we'll have to take care of it. You handle the details, but, right now, we have other matters."

"Oh? Such as?"

"A railroad, the Atcheson, Topeka, and Santa Fe is pushing rails into Newton. Newton is sixty-five miles south of here. Cattlemen down south aren't going to bring stock this far north when they can cut miles and time from a drive. Abilene is going to lose out. We are going to have to change operations, but," Slick Comer grinned, "we still got a few months to go. Better make good use of what time we got left. We know the country here."

"All right." Ten's linear, sallow face seemed to darken, but he allowed an enigmatic smile. "So what do we do next?"

"There's a big herd on the way now. It's about thirty miles from here, near the Republican River."

"I know that one, the Long Bar X brand."

Comer continued without a break in countenance, but his mind was alive. So, Ten had been looking around, eh? He was capable of running the show, and was sizing things up in his own mind. Well, Comer smiled inwardly, Stace had paid a recent visit, and was waiting on word from him to act.

"Yes," Comer didn't miss a beat, "the Long Bar X. I think we better hit it. Can you get the men ready?"

Ten thought a minute, "Two days. They are scattered."

"That's risky. The herd will be only ten, maybe fifteen miles from town. Too close. People might be poking around. Can't take a chance."

"All right. I can get them tomorrow. The herd will still be twenty miles off, so we'll be out of sight pretty good."

"Sierra and Jord still hiding?"

"At the soddy. We are paying them, so let's get our money's worth. I'll keep them out of town."

Comer was thoughtful. "Word's out about the EW job. The Long Bar X will have more guards. Will thirty men be enough?"

"Yes." Ten shifted his long body to a more comfortable position. "I saw Stace with that

EW bunch, but we didn't get him. I want that one, Comer."

"You know him?"

"I know his reputation and figure to change that."

Slick Comer was full of secret smiles. Two professionals against each other. If they both died, he'd be way ahead. He still owed Stace a thousand, but dead men don't collect. And Ten would be six feet under.

He asked, "What about the boy, Red they call him? He knows too much."

"I got ideas for that one." Ten's cold eyes lit up. "Very definite ideas about him and Stace."

For a second, Slick Comer felt a stab of alarm. He didn't want Ten shooting Stace in the back. Stace was his hole card, his protection. But his momentary nerves settled quickly. Ten might shoot the boy in the back, but not Stace. Ten would face the other man straight on. It was a matter of pride.

"Have a drink to success, Ten?"

"Pour it out."

Comer poured, and they toasted.

To your death after this job, Comer thought to himself.

I'll bury you, promised Ten silently, *after the Long Bar X stock is sold.*

"To our continued success," said Comer aloud.

"I'll always drink to that," agreed Ten, and his hard features broke into the warmest smile.

They finished a second drink, and then left, Ten to round up the needed men, Comer to find a buyer for 'his' cattle. There was one in particular he wanted to contact, Jones. Jones never looked at brands too closely.

As soon as the men departed, the office fell into the silence of disuse of offices everywhere. It remained so for several minutes, the dead air only slightly tainted with the varnishy odor of wooden cabinets and the oak desk.

Into this eerie silence a sound crept forth, a tentative sound from behind a closet door. Seconds later, the figure of a man stepped carefully from the closet and into the room. He closed the door carefully and stood there pondering. The man was Stace.

He had left the boy, Red, an hour before, wanting to investigate on his own. The way he figured it, if Comer was a suspect, there could be something in his records that would show him up. But how to get into those records? By the direct method, of course, go to them. It was not likely Comer would open his files, so

Stace took the alternative, as any good Pinkerton agent would. He let himself into the office without a problem—whoever locked a door in Abilene?—and was busy examining files, when he heard the men approaching.

There were two alternatives: he could stand and try to explain, which would mean a fight, or he could hide. Fighting wouldn't have helped, because he had not found anything in the files that would be useful. Comer was good at keeping books, and his records were all straight forward. He'd purchased so many cattle for such and such a price on a certain date. Stace was certain Comer ran his legitimate business parallel to the illegal business. The rustled cattle were probably not recorded in any way. The only door open to the rustled herds would be bank accounts. Did Comer and Ten's account swell suddenly for no obvious reason? These herds were no doubt sold, mainly, to shady dealers. The cattle selling and buying business was big, and wide open. Questions were not asked as long as the animals had brands.

Stace hadn't got as far as the bank accounts yet. He wanted to keep his identity secret. Getting to the accounts meant he'd have to reveal his connection to the Pinkertons.

Comer and Ten would be alerted, and that wouldn't do.

Stace smiled, a sardonic outlet reflecting his inner emotions. He had been an outlaw, was still an outlaw, because he'd contracted with Comer to kill Ten. It was a job he undertook without compunction, considering the kind of man Ten was. He was being well-paid for the mission, but after it was over, he planned to leave behind the mercenary jobs and continue with the Pinkertons as an undercover agent. He was now an outlaw with a change of heart, and a man who knew the inside of the outside.

Stace was playing a triple game. He was a favored employee of the EW ranch, a hired gun for Comer, and a detective. So far, it had gone well, and would, he hoped, go even better tomorrow night.

He left the building and went to the marshal's office for a talk.

Later, he rushed to Gail's quarters in the hotel. He'd heard about her from Marshal Smith. She and Brad were in the lobby, heading for a restaurant.

"I heard you been gunning for a couple of snakes," he said abruptly.

"Something like that."

Brad was standing next to the girl, and Stace sensed a new closeness between the two.

"You've got Brad," he told Gail, "but, don't forget, you have me too."

Gail smiled. "Thank you, Stace. I'll remember."

Stace then told the pair what he had been up to in the office, but didn't mention he was a Pinkerton agent or a hired gun for Comer. The time was still not right.

"You heard them making plans?" Brad was enormously pleased. Here was a rope he could hang on to.

"Yep, for the Long Bar X brand, and for you and me."

"Us?"

"They intend to kill us as well as Gail and Red.

"No tongues to wag, right?"

"What savages they are," Gail said.

"For them, it's just business."

The girl shuddered.

Stace added, "We'll get them tomorrow night." He told them about his talk with the marshal.

"He'll be on hand?" Tucker wanted to clinch the nail.

"With a full crew."

Both Tucker and Gail smiled.

"Good," nodded the EW trail boss, "I want them bad. I want to get them if it's the last thing I ever do."

Gail nodded, and whispered, almost in prayer, "I hope my father will be watching this. He deserves it."

Chapter Eight

When Stace left Red alone to conduct his private business, the boy felt strange. This was the first time he had been alone since Brad put him on the payroll. For the past months he'd been surrounded by cattle and lively cowboys on the trail, and since that terrible massacre, he had drawn close to the survivors, Brad and Stace, and now, Gail.

Suddenly, there were no adult eyes watching him, no adult management. He felt in his pockets. He'd been paid off for his part of the drive and had a bunch of banknotes and silver tucked away. For the first time in his young life, he owned real money.

Abilene was a town full of enticing

beckonings. There was the Devil's Addition, which was not so much a mystery to the boy as a perplexity. He was a frontier youth, accustomed to the rough social customs of a drifting population. He knew what went on in the Addition, but what he didn't understand was why the place should be named after Lucifer. After all, from what he'd heard, a fellow could have a great time in the Addition. Why bring the devil into it?

There were other places in town he figured as devilish, but they enjoyed a good reputation. Three bars in particular were favored, the Alamo, the Bullshed, and the Applejack. Abilene, after the manner of its peers in the West, was wide open. You could get about anything you wanted here.

Red jingled his coins and felt the wrinkled softness of the paper money. He eyed the Applejack. He had been in bars before, but never had money to spend. He was a tall youngster, hefty for his age, and could pass as a man, if the observer didn't look too closely. Not that it mattered to the crusty bartenders, he guessed, as long as he had money to spend.

Trying to look as old as possible by putting on a serious face and furrowing his brow, he sauntered toward the Applejack. Noise issued from its open doors. Somebody was troubling a piano with something like music. Though it was only ten in the morning, Red heard girls laughing, and the clink of glasses. But, so what? There was a party going on in Abilene 365 days a year.

He closed in on the Applejack, outwardly confident, inwardly hesitant. His heart was racing, and his palms were sweaty. He almost wished he wasn't doing what he was doing, but a force kept him on the path toward that yawning door.

Across the street, Ten watched as the red-headed youth sauntered toward the bar. He had often observed the boy in the company of Stace. The two had been together constantly since arriving in Abilene. He knew Stace was teaching the boy how to use his six-gun properly. He had had opportunities to bushwack Stace, but Ten had an inverted pride; he would want to face the other man one-on-one. The boy, however, was too tempting to ignore.

He crossed the street. When Red's booted feet stepped up on the boardwalk in front of the Applejack, Ten swung around in front of him.

The boy stopped abruptly, staring at the man before him. He had never seen Ten before, but he sensed danger. There was a look in the man's eyes and a mention in the solid stance of the slim body that stood so still that was threatening.

He started around the menace but was stopped with, "Come with me, boy."

"Nope," and Red continued around the man.

A hand flashed out, and struck him across the cheek. Red gasped, flushed, and doubled his fists for a swing. He stood as tall as Ten and outweighed him by fifty pounds. Ten ignored the doubled fists. Instead, he placed a long-fingered hand on the butt of his pistol.

"You come quietly," he hissed through tight lips, "or I'll kill you."

Red froze. "But you got no cause," he stammered. "Who are you?"

"Never mind who I am. And I can cook up a reason for killing you. You drew on me, see?" He glanced at Red's firearm hanging by the boy's side. "I got a reputation, and you're a punk looking for glory. You tried me, and I beat you to the draw. It's been done before." A note of pride. "But nobody has beat me yet, and they never will."

The young cowboy knew he was trapped, but in spite of his fright, he was puzzled.

"What do you want me for?"

"That's for me to know, kid. Get moving."

"Where?"

"We'll get our horses, and you're going to spend a few days in the country. You'll like it," Ten finished sarcastically.

On their way to the stables, Red kept an eye open for Stace, or Tucker, or even Gail Fanchy. But they were all occupied elsewhere, and he left town prisoner to a stranger.

They rode for what seemed like forever to Red. Finally, they pulled up at a little soddy southwest of town. There were several men present, tough looking gents, who, thought Red, probably squeezed little birds to death for fun.

"What you got there?" one of them rasped. He had a shock of greasy, blond hair.

"A little insurance," was the reply.

"In-sur-ence?" Another man was curious. "What's that, boss?" He had a swarthy complexion with a deep facial scar and a droopy, black mustache.

"That means our job tomorrow night," Ten told him, "will be protected, Sierra."

"Ah," the swarthy one smiled, wrinkling his scar into an ugly configuration, "good, good." He leered at Red. "Welcome, boy, to our little home."

There were several others present, and they laughed at the 'little home' phrase. They smelled of sweat, grime, and raw whiskey.

"We going tomorrow for sure?"

This was from the blond man.

Tucker's Law

"I said so, Jord." Ten's voice was steel.

"Yeah, sure, don't get cranky, but look at this place. A man can take only so much of it."

"I want you all sober tomorrow night. Any drunks will be dealt with, you understand?"

"Yeah, yeah," was the general rumble. Still, they had all seen Ten kill Ruffy in cold blood. That memory, alone, put a damper on rebellion. They would all be sober.

"You be ready by sundown, hear?" Ten spoke sharply, making his wish very clear.

"We'll be waiting, boss," said the mustached man, Sierra.

Ten nodded. "You're in charge, you and Jord there. I'll hold you two responsible."

"You do that," grunted Sierra, "an' if anything goes wrong, what you gonna do?"

Ten backed off a bit. He was facing a Gila monster of a man. "I leave it to you, and Jord," he said smoothly, "because I can depend on you. I know you. I don't know the others well enough. I trust you and Jord, Sierra."

He didn't show his secret dislike for the two for failing to kill Gail Fanchy. Ten hated ineptness. But the two were good at what they did most of time and had proved it before, so he let the failure go. He needed the pair and others like them.

"Yeah, all right, boss, don't worry." Sierra turned a quizzical eye on Red. "What about him?"

"Just hang on to him. I want him kept under wraps."

Sierra took a closer look. "Well, if he ain't one of 'em from the EW job!"

"That's right," Ten admitted, knowing that Sierra's recognition sealed the boy's fate. The kid knew too much now and would have to be killed later.

He left the men to water his horse at a nearby trickle of a stream, probably the only reason the soddy had been built in an otherwise uncompromising landscape of buckbrush, clump grass, rocks and gritty sand. When he returned, he found the gang hazing Red. There were eight men in this group, one of similar groups placed around the country when big jobs were at hand. Anticipating action soon, Sierra and Jord, along with two or three others, had gathered the men together already. That was one reason Ten wanted to keep the pair. They knew the routine.

The men had taken the boy's hat, and were trying it on. It was a new sombrero, with a flat crown, the kind that Stace wore. The hat was one of the first things Red bought after payday.

The gang was passing it from hand to hand trying it on, making remarks like, "My, don't I look sweet?" Or, "Just like a stage actor, how handsome!" Or, "This ought to get the gals all right," and so on.

Red simply stood in the center of them, a lamb surrounded by wolves. He had the good sense not to object. Maybe the moment would pass. Ten had taken his pistol, so there was nothing he could do, anyway. He projected a brave front, but he was secretly terrified. He was totally aware of what was happening. He knew he could be killed for knowing too much now. They couldn't afford to let him go.

Ten departed for Abilene. His next task was to convince Comer that he had done the right thing. He didn't push his horse, a buckskin gelding, because he wasn't in any hurry. The buckskin was a good horse, swift and sure-footed, and possessed an eerie ability to see in the dark, and Ten wanted to use him the next night, so he rode him easy to keep him fresh.

He reached forward and patted the tawny, arched neck.

"You get me through tomorrow," he said, "and I'll put you out to pasture in the best field around."

Though Ten would not admit it to anybody, he

liked the horse, and was actually so fond of it that he felt as if there were a bond between them.

When he got back into town, he caught Slick Comer in his office. Comer was in a foul mood.

"Where you been?" he snarled. "We need to talk!"

Ten's voice grew very soft. "Don't strike on me, Comer."

"Look, we got plans to go over. We should ride out to where those cattle are and get the lay of the land. Got to know for sure where to hide them. We got work to do, friend."

"Well, *friend,* I have been working. For one thing, the men are already in place. We could go tonight."

"Oh?" Comer was unpleasantly surprised. Ten had been anticipating him?

"Also," Ten added, "I got us insurance."

"Insurance?" Comer was puzzled. "What you mean?"

"I got the boy."

"The boy?"

"Yeah, that kid with the EW outfit. He hangs around with that fellow, Stace. I told you I had plans for him."

"But why? The boy belongs to the enemy camp. They'll come after him. I don't like that, Ten."

"Didn't think you would. Don't care much what you think, but look at it this way. The boy will keep Tucker and Stace away from us while we," a thin smile here, "work."

"And how will that help? I think Stace, at least, would come after him." He had also observed the close friendship between the two.

"No, I'm going to see to it he keeps them all away."

"How?"

Ten pulled a folded paper from his pocket and showed it to Comer. A scrawled note read, "Stay away. Do anything silly like interfere, and the boy is dead."

Comer studied the note, and slowly recognized its merit, but it was a different merit than Ten saw. Stace would search for the boy, regardless. He would hunt Ten down to rescue the boy, and the two gunmen would face each other. And what would come next? The inevitable, of course. He allowed a smile.

"Yes," he said, "practically opens all the doors, right?"

Ten nodded. But he, too, realized the fallacy of the note. He knew it would bring Stace to him, and he knew, as did Stace, there would be a showdown. He would kill the man, and possibly Comer at the same time.

A plot within a plot within a plot.

Both Ten and Comer smiled. All was working as each wanted.

Later that day, Gail Fanchy found the note; it had been slipped under her door.

Chapter Nine

Gail quickly found Brad Tucker and Stace. She showed them the note.

"So," was Tucker's comment, "we are now playing a larger game."

"I could go after Ten," Stace commented, "it's me he wants, I'm pretty sure."

Gail looked at him. "Why you?"

"Well," it had to come out now, "I have this reputation, Gail."

"Ah?" The girl looked at Brad.

Brad explained, and Gail took it all. She nodded, but said, "I don't want you hurt, or put you outside the law on account of the EW loss."

"As Brad pointed out," Stace replied

carefully, "it's a larger game now, or, at least, different."

"But," the girl pointed to the note, "we don't know if it is from that man. It isn't signed."

"But we can use an educated guess," Tucker said. "He and his partner, Slick Comer, know that we guess right."

"So, now what?"

Stace was clearly agitated. He'd grown close to Red, a son he'd never had. In his life, following the pathways he had chosen, or which had been forced on him, there had been no time for a family. But with Red around, he had experienced feelings he never knew existed; he was getting a taste of fatherhood, just a taste but he had warmed to it.

"I'll never forgive myself if something happens to that boy!" Stace was angry. "If only I hadn't left him!"

"It was important you did," Tucker reminded him quietly. "Your idea of looking at bank accounts might help nail Comer and his deadly partner. You did what you had to do."

Stace had suggested that much without revealing his Pinkerton connection.

He nodded. "I know all that, but it doesn't change the fact that an innocent boy is paying a heavy price."

They had gathered in Gail's room at the

hotel, and a gloomy silence fell over the three. Tucker went to the window and studied the street, as if, somehow, he could divine a solution. He watched Marshal Smith clump past on the boardwalk below.

"We better tell Smith," Brad said, "the more in on this, the better."

The lawman was in his office. Tucker did the talking, and the marshal listened carefully. It was understood among the three friends that Smith didn't trust Stace.

"You sure that note is from Ten?" Smith questioned. None of the three noticed a tightening of the lawman's jaw when he asked.

"Who else?" Stace broke in. "He knows we saw him during the raid. He's fighting us."

"Him and Comer," added Brad.

"I ought to go hunting," Stace said.

The marshal was noncommittal; Tucker pressed the point.

"They took the boy to a hideout I'm pretty sure, but you're right, Stace. Let's hunt in town first. We might find somebody who has answers."

"I'll put a couple of men on it," Smith offered, "but I don't have much time for this. You'll be on your own mostly."

Then he added, "What about tomorrow night? Are you coming?"

"If we do, and are seen by Ten and Comer, the boy will be in danger," Stace cut in.

"Let's make a decision after we complete a town search," suggested Gail.

Tucker glanced at the girl, "How do you want to do this? We should split up to cover more ground, but I'd feel better if you were with me."

She nodded. "I'll go with you."

The marshal and his men decided to search the downtown area, the bars, and the Devil's Addition. Tucker and Gail would visit the livery stables, hotels, and restaurants. Stace would look into the nearby herds, the stockyards, and even the railroad box cars.

"You never know," he growled, "maybe you're right, Brad, maybe they are out of town—but you never know the mind of a crook."

They met back in Marshal Smith's office after several hours. Abilene wasn't that large.

"They've left for parts unknown," concluded Tucker.

"We still have to make a decision about tomorrow night," said Gail. "Are we going with the marshal?"

"The way I see it," Stace's voice was tight, "that could be the same as signing Red's death certificate. Ten is after me. If I don't get him, he'll hold the boy hostage to make an escape. When he's safe, he'll kill the boy."

"So what's your decision?" The marshal asked.

"We better hold back," said Brad reluctantly.

The other two nodded.

The marshal, in keeping with custom, made it known he had already sent one of his deputies, a man named Waddy, to warn the Long Bar X herd people. He wondered how Waddy was doing.

It was not going well for Deputy Waddy, who was twenty or thirty miles from town, wandering off the main trail by accident. During one wrong turn, he stumbled across a soddy. He was surprised, not knowing such existed in this part of the world. As a boy, he and his family had built one in Dakota Territory, and lived in it for several years while his father had tried his hand at cattle ranching. The soddy, though cramped, had been warm in winter, cool in summer, and he remembered the hut with fondness. His mother had kept the place clean and filled the dirt interior with the scent of her delicious freshly baked bread.

When he spied this soddy, he approached

and dismounted. He felt somehow on home ground, half expecting to see his long dead mother in the doorway.

"I say there!" he called.

A tall, thin man with narrow eyes and long fingers stepped forth. The deputy recognized him as Ten. He knew nothing of the recent search for him.

"I need a drink of your water," he said.

"There's a stream full of it," replied Ten, "help yourself."

A slick-haired man joined Ten, and the deputy recognized him as Comer.

"I say," he offered conversationally, "you fellers is a long way out in nowhere."

Ten and Comer both recognized the deputy—they knew all the lawmen in Abilene and other towns in the region. Others in the soddy stepped to the door, Red among them. When he saw the deputy, he shouted, "Help! I'm being held here! I've been kidnapped!"

He started to struggle through the doorway, but a sharp blow from Ten tumbled him back.

"Say," the deputy began.

But that was his last word.

Ten had pulled his .44 and shot him through the heart. One shot and the lawman collapsed, struggled in violent death throes, and then lay still forever.

"Good shot," approved Slick Comer. "Fifty feet, and you got him square."

Ten nodded and released one of his thin-lipped smiles. Then he snarled at Red, "You, kid, keep your mouth shut, or you'll get the same. Now get a shovel, and bury the corpse, before it gets to stinking."

Red gave a white-faced stare at the huddled, bloodied figure of what had been a living man and threw up.

Others at the soddy expressed no opinion. They had learned to keep quiet.

Chapter Ten

Marshal Smith was concerned. Waddy had not yet returned, and though the man's whereabouts didn't concern him so much what he might have learned did. If Waddy had found out anything damning about him, would the deputy come back to Abilene or tell the authorities in another town?

That would never do. As marshal, he'd worked long and hard in a dangerous profession, and he did not want his reputation damaged now. So what if he was in on Ten and Comer's schemes? What if he did get a cut of the rustled cattle profits? He was about to retire. He was, at sixty, too old to fight the young toughs, and he needed the money. A lawman's pay was barely enough to keep bread on the table.

As the days wore on, the marshal became more nervous, but, on schedule, he gathered his men together—six, not including himself and four of them were specially deputized. There was safety in numbers, but Marshal Tom Smith wanted a different safety; numbers made him seem he was doing everything possible to solve the rustlings and killings. He would, of course, deliberately lead his men in the wrong direction. He knew where the soddy was.

Tucker, Gail, and Stace were in the marshal's office as the law departed.

"I wish we were going with you," Tucker commented.

The marshal nodded, "But you ain't, so just keep your eyes open here. We'll get ahold of you when we get back."

He and his men trotted their horses from town across the rail tracks, skirting the cowpens. Marshal Smith's face was drawn and dark with his thoughts.

"I'd give anything to be going with them," muttered Tucker, his own face taut with the strain.

"Me too," said Gail fiercely. "I hope they take those murderers alive. I want to see them in court. I want to see them hang! I want them to hurt before they die and pay for the terrible crimes they committed."

"Amen to that," agreed Stace. He was not only thinking of the girl's loss of her father, but his own loss. Red. Where was the boy, where had be been hidden? Was he alive? Should he dare accompany the marshal and risk the boy getting killed?

Stace shivered at the thought and left the office abruptly. "I can't hang around," he said, "Got to move a bit. Think I'll take my horse out for a ride."

"We'll headquarter here," said Brad. "Check in from time to time." He nodded at a deputy, a tall man with a long, pockmarked face who'd been left behind to take care of emergencies. "Jake will know where we are."

After Stace left, Brad took Gail to a restaurant for coffee.

"Things sure got turned around," he said, as they sipped the black, steaming brew. "I figured to be in on this all the way."

The girl nodded. "I know. I feel the same."

She looked at the man opposite her. She hadn't known him long, but she was in love with him. He was relaxed in the chair, his long frame sort of sprawled out. He seemed for all the world like a man who hadn't a care in the world. But his face, she noted, was pale under the tan, and the lines around his mouth were more deeply etched. His eyes, usually clear, were clouded from lack of sleep. The situation was having its effect. He'd lost good men to the killers.

"Don't worry . . ." she began, while Tucker simultaneously voiced the same words.

They stopped, startled, and laughed softly, the first laugh they'd enjoyed in some time.

"I guess we are in tune," observed Brad.

"Does that mean anything?" Gail parried.

"It does to me."

"Me too."

Tucker leaned across the table and kissed her.

"Why, Brad," was the delighted response, "kissing in public. What will people say?"

"Are you worried?"

"Yes." She kissed him in return. "But not much."

Brad grasped her hand gently.

"I'm sorry we had to meet under the circumstances we did, but I'm glad we met."

"Yes."

"I've never had a steady girlfriend before," there was a hint of teasing in his voice. "If I don't behave right, please let me know."

"What would the right behavior be? I've never had a steady boyfriend, either, so how would I know?"

He sighed. "I guess we'll just have to learn

together." He kissed her again. "I realize this is improper behavior. Will you make a note of it?"

"I don't have a pencil or paper."

"What kind of a woman doesn't carry paper and pencil with which to make emergency notes?"

"Feckless."

"Am I really talking to a feckless person?"

"Worse. I'm also hopeless."

"Hopeless?"

"Hopelessly in love."

Sudden pain clouded the girl's eyes. "Why are we talking like this when men are riding to their deaths maybe? And while Red is in trouble, or . . . or . . ."

Brad rose and caught her in his arms. They left the restaurant and walked slowly toward the marshal's office.

"We were talking like that," he said, "because we both think like that. We tease naturally, but I think, also, we're talking that way to ease our minds of what's happening. Stace went for a ride. You and I act silly."

Gail nodded. "How I hate this waiting. Should we do something? Go for a ride too?"

Brad saw the need in her, the need to keep her mind from dwelling too much on darkness. They saddled up and walked their horses from town. They put the noise and confusion of the streets behind them in fifteen minutes.

As they rode, they talked to each other in intimate terms, learning about each other, fuelling the love they felt. They rode side by side, holding hands, and if they met somebody on the road they held on, but made way for the stranger. They rode until the sun grew uncomfortably hot, and then they returned. Smoky, Tucker's gelding, seemed to pick up a bit, and his rider offered a comment.

"Smoky, you walking feed bag, you think oats are waiting, eh?"

And the horse waggled his ears as he always did when Brad spoke to him.

"Brilliant animal," he said to Gail, and she nodded.

"Any horse," she agreed, "who knows how to handle the hand that handles the oat bag is brilliant."

"You mean that?"

"Every word."

"Smoky will be proud."

"We are being silly again."

"Yes!" Brad slammed a fist into his hand. "I hate this waiting. I should be there. This is my battle!"

"And," the girl prompted, "mine."

"Yes, of course."

They stabled their horses and returned to the marshal's office. Stace was there alone.

"I don't suppose you've heard anything," Brad said.

"We just have to wait," was the curt reply. This brought a quick glance from Brad. "Sorry," muttered Stace, "you know how it is."

When night fell, they took turns eating. First Stace, then Tucker and Gail. Jake opened an empty cell for them so they could rest on the cots. At midnight, Stace stretched out. Another deputy by the name of Bill, who had a great, handlebar mustache, relieved Jake. Gail rested on a cot, refusing to return to her room, even though both Brad and Stace said they'd let her know of any news.

Just at sunup, they saw riders approaching—Marshal Smith and his deputies, all six of them.

"I don't see any prisoners," observed Stace.

"Maybe none were taken," put in Gail.

"Could be, but I can't see seven lawmen coming back, not with Ten shooting," Brad said.

"The marshal looks pretty grim," Gail pointed out. "Just look at him."

Indeed, the man's features, roughed up from years of exposure to the prairie's weather moods and human cussedness, were set in a hard mold. His eyes were narrowed and fixed on the office. They never blinked, not once, as they advanced across the boardwalk. His boots made a thonk-thonk sound in the clear, still air.

He pushed the door open and confronted them, a tough man, whose toughness was now wide open for all to see.

"I'm glad you're all here," he said through clenched teeth. "Makes it easier to arrest you."

Brad stopped cold. He eyed the lawman, and could see the marshal was not fooling.

The deputies crowded into the room.

"What do you mean arrest us?" Brad was at a loss.

"I mean just that." He looked at Gail with hard eyes. "Sorry, ma'am, you and that snake, Stace, are included."

Stace stiffened. "We've done nothing."

"Oh, not for the last twenty-four hours, maybe, but you sure worked mischief before then."

"I don't get this."

"Then, get this: none of them Long Bar X cattle were around, not even a yearling. Nothing! Do you understand that?" The marshal's voice rose with emotion, signaling there was more to come. "And not a living man there."

After a shocked silence, Gail's voice was faint. "What do you mean not a living man?"

"I mean they were all dead, that's what I mean, Missy!"

Brad entered with, "The same pattern as with your herd, Gail, and mine." He turned to the marshal. "Why should we be connected to that? Miss Fanchy and I have both been hurt by those killers. Why would we join them?"

The marshal shook his head. "Who knows why? Who knows what goes on in the minds of crooks or people who want to get even for something they've lost. I'm not a fortune teller." He glowered at Stace. "But if you keep company with rats like this, you could be talked into anything, even if he is a Pinkerton man."

Brad and Gail stared at Stace in surprise.

"Pinkerton?" Brad said.

Stace nodded. "I was sent here to investigate the GF rustlings, as requested by Smith here."

The marshal interjected with, "I sure never requested you. I wanted a law-abiding man."

"I am law-abiding, Marshal." Stace winced inwardly, remembering his appointment with Ten through Slick Comer.

"No," decided the marshal, "you ain't. Not you, or your kind. I've never known a gunman to reform." His voice tightened. "If Tucker here and Miss Fanchy didn't tell the rustlers about our proposed raid last night, then you did—for a cut of the profits, if I don't miss my guess."

He swung on Brad and Gail.

"They was a few Long Bar X horses grazing around, that's how we knew the bodies were from that ranch. Both of you know how it's done, and if you didn't stop Stace from going out there to warn Comer and Ten, you should have. You are guilty by association, both of you."

The marshal turned to his men. "Take their guns."

Swift as a striking rattler, Stace's weapon flashed into view.

"Don't any of you move," he said, and his voice was deadly. "We are innocent, but you got in your head we are guilty, Marshal. We can't prove we aren't if we're in jail, so we'll stay free."

Brad pulled his own weapon, realizing, fully, that Stace was right. In jail, they were guilty.

"Head for the cells," Stace ordered the lawmen.

In minutes, the law was locked tight, and the three fled. They raced to the stable, saddled up, and headed away. They heard the marshal and others shouting for help, but they cleared town without pursuit.

"Now where?" Stace shouted.

"Just away," decided Tucker. "Just remember where we've been, so we can keep our bearings. It is time," he added grimly, "for us to take matters into our own hands." He gave a short laugh. "Tucker's law!"

"Suits me," agreed Gail, "just fine."

Without knowing it, they were pointed in the direction of the soddy where Red was being held. It was necessary to push their horses hard, while keeping wary eyes on the rear trail.

"They probably think we took one of the main roads," said Brad. "There will be thirty men hunting us down in half an hour."

"They think we're guilty for sure, running like this." Gail was rueful.

"What else could we do?" Stace asked. "They planned a party for us, Gail, a necktie party, know what I mean?"

"Without any real proof?"

"Marshal Smith had all the proof he needed." Stace pointed at himself. "Me."

Gail nodded. "I know we had to escape, but," her voice was loaded with frustration, "life sure takes some funny turns."

"Not funny like in laughing," added Brad.

He looked at the girl. She had courage. She was not only beautiful, but ready to follow whatever course was necessary in life. She was right. Life took some funny turns, but she went along with them and made the best of them. An ordinary girl would have collapsed in grief after her father's death. Gail took matters in her own hand, determined to find the killers. He smiled at her, and she returned the smile. She wanted his arms around her, and he wanted her in them, but with Stace looking on, it was not exactly a good time. They settled for smiles and rode their horses steadily.

All three rode side by side with plenty of room.

Brad glanced at Stace. "A Pinkerton man, eh?"

Stace nodded.

"I'd have never guessed."

"You weren't supposed to."

"Pretty clever way of getting on my payroll. Were those men you were battling for real?"

Stace grinned. "Oh, yes, that was real enough, all right. They were owl-hoot boys, and I rode with them once. They wanted me back. Actually, I was going to ask you for a job, but it worked out just as well."

"And here I thought I was helping a poor critter out of work."

"I kept no secrets—well, except for being a detective. You know all about me."

"Yep. Got to admit that. Is that all you are, Stace?"

Stace was startled. "What you mean by that?"

"No more surprises in you?"

"You mean did I somehow tip off Ten and Comer?"

"No. I know you didn't. You were with us the whole the time." Brad hesitated. He was walking on conjecture here. "But at times you seemed preoccupied, like there was something unpleasant in your mind."

Stace studied the other man. Had he been so obvious? His hiring out to Comer to kill Ten had been in his thoughts, naturally. He was waiting for word from Comer to do the job. The ambiguity of his life—trail hand, Pinkerton, hired killer, would give anybody a wrinkled brow, but he thought he'd covered pretty well.

"No," he lied, "there's nothing else. You know the whole thing."

Brad nodded. He wasn't sure that "No" was all truth, but he did feel he could still trust Stace. That was what was necessary for now.

The three traveled in silence, the miles passing beneath the hoofs of their horses. Then, without warning, beside the murmur of a small creek, the soddy rose up.

"There's somebody here too," muttered Stace.

Several horses were hobbled in a spot of grass.

"I've seen that one before," Gail pointed to a roan. Suddenly, she gasped. "He carried that greasy blond man. One of those who . . ."

She didn't have to finish her sentence.

Dismounting, the three crept to the hut, guns drawn. Stace went to the rough, plank door, and called, "Anybody who is in there, speak your piece."

A voice answered, a sort of squall, an adolescent howl, followed by a slapping sound, and a hissed, "Shut up!"

Stace raised his voice. "Red, are you in there?"

The reply was muffled. There were distinct sounds of a scuffle. Stace realized if the voice was Red's, the boy was in great danger. He bashed the door open with his shoulder, and plunged into the gloom.

A shot boomed, and Stace felt the bullet whiz by his shoulder. He fired at the orange flash of the gun, and a shadowy figure collapsed. Tucker and Gail rushed through the door. More shots bloomed in the semi-darkness. Figures stood out more plainly as their eyes grew accustomed to the shadows.

"Give it up!" Stace cried over the roar of battle.

"Not on your life!" cried Jord. He aimed at Stace coolly, then a shadow tackled him from the side. It was Red. The two, grappling, crashed over and got tangled in the crude furniture. Stace rushed to them and dragged them apart. In the meantime, Tucker and Gail kept firing at the others.

Jord leaped up crying, "I knew we should've kilt you, kid!" He turned his weapon on Red, but just then another shot deafened the small room, and Jord jerked to a stop. He glared at Stace, muttered, "Well, by heaven . . ." and then sagged against the dirt wall, hung there for a moment, and sank to the floor.

Stace stared at the man without sympathy. "You'll never threaten young ones again, partner."

The fighting ceased. There were groans from the opposing side, and there was, also, an eerie silence. Two figures were sprawled on the floor, resting in eternity. There were only two men left on their feet.

"Drop your guns," Brad ordered, and the orders were followed.

One of the men was wounded in the shoulder, the other stood dazed in the yard. The noise of weapons had left him, and the rest of them, deaf.

"What was that all about?" he demanded, shaky.

"You rustled Long Bar X cattle last night, didn't you?"

"Never heard of it."

"You also held the boy hostage."

"What boy?"

The man was belligerent.

"Me," said Red.

"Why would I do that? Weren't any of my doings."

Leaving him, with Gail as guard, Brad and Stace went back inside the soddy. Jord still had life in him.

"You rustled Long Bar X stock didn't you?"

Stace spoke quietly, almost gently, even though the man had tried to kill him. Stace was always gentle with the dying, even though he, himself, could have been on the receiving end of a bullet.

Jord looked at him through glazing eyes. "Is the kid dead?" he whispered.

"No."

Jord shook his head. "I knew he'd bring trouble." He was silent a moment, gasping for air.

"Tell us," Brad came in, "Did you rustle Long Bar X cattle last night? Don't go and die with a lie on your lips, man."

Jord coughed, and blood dribble down his chin. Making an effort, he managed a faint, "Yes."

At that moment, Gail glanced through the door, and stiffened.

"That's one of them," she said, "who tried to kill me."

"Who was the other?" Brad demanded.

"Sierra," Jord muttered

"That will be the last time you ever pull something like that," growled Brad, who was not gentle. "Now, did you do the rustling?"

Jord nodded, his strength ebbing.

"You and who else?"

Jord bobbed his head at the men outside, and those who lay so still nearby.

"We were all in on it, except for the kid, who was tied up in here. Yeah . . . me and Comer, and that gunman, Ten . . ."

Suddenly, Jord gave a hard cough of blood, and sagged. He was dead.

Stace and Brad stood up. "Well, we know more than we did, now," said Stace.

Brad nodded, but said, "I don't know how much good it's going to do, though."

"What you mean? This should get us off the hook."

"Maybe." Brad turned to Red. "Did Ten and Comer kidnap you?"

"Ten did. He cornered me in town, and I couldn't get away." The boy shivered. "I think he was going to use me as bait to get to you, Stace."

"Yeah, he was probably going to draw me here, after last night was over."

"What a rotten bunch," said Gail in horror.

Brad pointed to a long mound of fresh dirt. "Who does that belong to?"

"That there is a deputy marshal. Ten shot him dead, and I had to bury him. Ugh."

Red was close to tears from the shock of it all.

"I have never," he said, "been up against anything like this in my life, and I never want to again."

"Then," said Stace, "don't learn too much about pistols, boy."

Red didn't understand.

"Live by the pistol, and die by it, son, like the deputy."

"But he was only standing there," said Red, "and Ten shot him down in cold blood."

"The deputy did carry a gun," Stace pointed out, "and, lawman or not, the rule holds for all."

Red nodded. "You trying to tell me something, Stace?"

"You know I am."

A groan from a wounded man brought them back to the scene.

"We have to get him to a doctor," said Gail, "and him," she pointed to the other survivor, "to jail."

They managed to tie the wounded outlaw upright in his saddle, then all five headed for Abilene.

"This should clear us." Gail was relieved. "We can get the law to trust us now."

"I wonder," said Brad. "I wonder."

His doubt exasperated Stace and Gail.

"Well, why not?" demanded the girl.

"Let's get on," was the enigmatic response. "We'll know soon enough."

Chapter Eleven

The Marshal had long lived in a dangerous profession. His long life was due to suspicion, and a careful reading of the human condition. Most people, he found, were not to be trusted when they dealt with the law directly. There seemed to be some kind of code that kept them from telling the whole truth.

He'd been a lawman in a variety of positions from an elected sheriff to a federally appointed marshal since he was in his early twenties. He took to the work naturally, as others might become businessmen or cowboys. The law was in his natural makeup. He served in whatever capacity was offered by the town be it Dodge City, Cheyenne, even as far north as Fort Benton. He'd known the likes of the Dalton boys, the Earps, John Wesley Hardin (one of the worst), and a "passel of others," as he put it. After having been duped by Billy the Kid, and wounded in range wars, he took no chances. He was admired by other lawmen and feared by the criminals.

The five drew up in front of his office, and dismounted, Brad and Stace helping the wounded man down.

"Well," the marshal stepped to the open door, "I see you found him. You all right, boy?"

He spoke without surprise. Little surprised him any more.

"Yes, sir."

Red could see that the marshal was not too friendly.

"Who took you?"

"It was Ten, who actually did it, but that man Comer backed him up."

"Do you have any proof Comer was in on it?"

"I was with them in a soddy where they held me. I heard them making plans for me."

"Plans, what plans?"

"I think they wanted Stace to track me down, use me as bait, and kill me in front of him."

"Why would they do that?"

"Ten wanted Stace was why. I think it was a

test of speed on the draw, or something like that."

"Why would they kill you?"

Red shrugged, then he said, "I saw Ten kill that deputy." The boy shuddered. "He simply shot him through the heart in cold blood, and said that business was business."

"You mean my deputy, Waddy?"

"I don't know his name, but I had to bury him."

The marshal was quiet for a moment. "Cold blood, eh?"

"Yes, sir."

Marshal Smith studied the boy for a moment, before answering firmly, "I don't believe you."

Brad and the others stared. "Why not?" Brad demanded.

"Because I know Stace and his kind. He's up to something, and he's got you to lie for him."

"That's not fair!" Gail snapped. "We rescued the boy and came to you with two gang members."

Red interrupted with, "They can tell you, Marshal. They were there too."

Smith turned to the outlaws. "Well, what about it?"

And true to the lawman's theory about crooks not telling the whole truth, both men lied.

"We wasn't there," said the wounded one. "We just got there when these people arrived, and started shooting at us."

"That's right," said the other. "We was just traveling through the country, and stopped to water our horses. Water is scarce in them parts."

The marshal said, "I know about that."

Brad was furious. "Listen, Red is correct. Why would he lie? Ten killed your deputy to protect their secrecy. They figured you was on to something and sent a deputy to look around. After that, they went for the Long Bar X cattle—probably a day or two early, knowing you'd look for Waddy."

"Yes," agreed Smith, "it all stacks up pretty well—for you."

Stace came in. "Look, I know you have it in for me, and others like me, but I'm a Pinkerton agent. I showed you my papers, so you got proof of that. Do you think they'd have just anybody on their payroll?"

"In a flash of lightning, if that somebody had a special talent, and you do."

"Such as?"

"Such as a quick-draw gunman like yourself. They figure you'd have ways of getting facts that honest men don't have." The marshal laughed, a bitter sound. "Oh, yes, they'd hire you." He paused. "Where is Waddy?"

"Still buried at the hut," supplied Brad.

Smith nodded at a couple of deputies, who had joined them. "Go after the body." He looked at the wounded man. "What about him?" he asked Brad.

"Well, lock him up!" exploded Brad, growing impatient with what he considered mulishness.

"On whose say? His?" He glared at Stace. "On the word of a gunman?"

"A Pinkerton," corrected Stace.

"Being one don't make you aces in my deck," was the salty response. There's something fishy here." He shrugged. "Lock him up boys," he said. "Can't hurt till this thing is over. Get the other one to the doctor. I got no idea what or who to believe in this whole shady mess." He gazed at the wounded man. "Who done this?"

Brad was cautious. "Maybe, I said maybe, one of us did it. And there's a few more for your boys to bury at the soddy. We found them dead. Jord was one of them. You know him." Jord was not a poplar man in Abilene, and had spent the night in jail for fighting more than once.

"Yeah, I know him."

Matters were going pretty much as Brad had expected them to go, but he wished he'd been wrong. With Stace in his bunch, though, he knew the marshal was not going to be all that happy with the way matters were turning out. He had chased outlaws all his life, and did not believe for an instant there was such a thing as a reformed gunman. But how about Ten? Surely Smith knew the man was a killer. Why didn't he believe Red about Ten's killing Waddy?

He was about to bring the matter up when Ten, along with Comer, arrived.

"Well, well," Comer greeted them with a sly smile, "what have we here?"

He'd seen the wounded man being led off and was now looking at Red with cleverly hidden surprise.

"Those are the men!" exclaimed the boy. "And that man there, Ten, he threatened to use his gun if I didn't go with him. The other one, he was at the soddy too."

Ten was as good at feigning surprise as Comer. "Never saw the lad in my life," he purred softly. "What's he jabbering about?"

"You know very well what he's talking about, mister." Brad was blunt. "We found him at the hut."

"Yeah," Stace's voice was strangely tender, "anybody who'd threaten a youngster is pretty yellow, I'd say."

There was a quick silence, as the two faced each other. Death rode the silent air.

"You been wanting this, that's why you took the kid," Stace went, "to get to me."

At that moment Brad noted something that gave an insight into the tangle in which their lives were caught. He saw Comer nod at Stace ever so quickly. That was a definite sign, but for what? Had the two worked something out? After all was said and done, he didn't really know much about Stace. Could it be that Comer was afraid of his partner? Had Stace been hired to kill Ten?

These were long thoughts, leaps, actually, but they made sense. That quick nod of Comer's had not been an accidental dip of the head. This would be a perfect setting for murder. A man's honor had been questioned. A quick draw to settle the insult was a reaction the West understood very well.

Stace's features turned as hard and smooth as polished granite. Ten followed the pattern to perfection. Both men knew exactly what they were doing, what moves to make next, like practiced ballet dancers. There was a ritual, and they both knew the steps. Provoke, insult, fight.

"I'm sorry you said that," Ten's voice was cushiony, almost inaudible. "I kind of admire you, Stace."

"You admire dog bones, my friend, because they are the cheapest cut of meat."

There was an electric tension now. You did not call a man yellow. You did not tell him he ate with the dogs.

Before they could finish their dance, though, Marshal Smith cut in.

"If either of you draws," he said, "and kills the other man, I'll jail the leftover, and see him hung. That clear?"

He drew his own weapon, and another deputy drew his.

"In fact," the marshal pointed out, "we might just have to shoot you both anyway, right, Charley?"

The deputy, a big raw-boned men, grinned.

"Right, Tom." He turned tight eyes on Stace. "I heard about you, jailbird."

That got Stace. "What about him?" he pointed at Ten. "He follows the same trade I did once."

Smith interrupted this exchange.

"I don't like him either," was the blunt response, "but he ain't been in jail, so he's not under suspicion like you." He eyed Ten. "I'd run you out of town in a minute. Just give me an excuse."

But Ten just grinned, a cold, thin-lipped crack, and waited silently. There were times when it was best not to talk. This was one of them.

Comer did the talking now.

"See here, Marshal, Ten isn't lilly white, sure, but we've been partners in cattle for a long time, and I can vouch for him."

"And who do you think you are?" was the grunted reply. I don't trust you, either, friend. You boys all behave like little gentlemen, you hear?"

Comer flushed.

"Now see here . . ." he began, but Smith cut him off with a wave of his pistol still out of its shiny, leather nest.

Brad told the marshal about Jord's confession.

The lawman snorted.

"You going to expect me to believe that? It's all hearsay, man. Your word against the statement of a dying man, don't mean a thing in court."

"You mean a man's last words won't hold up?"

"Sure, if I or one of my deputies heard them. I have no reason to trust you. You and Miss Gail here got personal reasons for wanting to hang Ten. Good ones, yes, but without proof."

Brad knew he was up against a wall. What the marshal said was correct; it was his word against that of a dying man, but word against word wasn't enough. He needed solid proof.

Suddenly, an idea flashed into Brad's mind.

"I'll have proof," he said to Smith. "Proof positive."

"Fine. You do that, and I'll believe you."

Later, over supper, during which Red ate twice as much as anybody since he'd been starved at the soddy, Gail asked, "What proof can you get, Brad?"

"Just wait," was the mysterious response. He wasn't about to reveal his idea. The less who knew, the better. "When Comer and Ten bring in 'their' stock, we'll get what we want."

"Might be a long wait," observed Stace.

"We have time."

Stace nodded.

"More of Tucker's law?"

"Maybe. Something like that."

Stace went on.

"Do you notice something about Marshal Smith?"

"What do you mean?"

"Well, he seems to be neutral in this matter, but I'm beginning to wonder."

Gail was interested. "So?"

"He's kept us out of the investigation, assuming Ten and I will fight. That's pretty thin, when I think about it."

"And?" from Brad.

"I wonder, this is just a 'wondering' mind

you, but is the good marshal hiding something?"

Brad settled back in his chair, and looked at Gail.

"Well," he said quietly. "The marshal is a good man, we all know that. Still, it has happened in the past . . ."

Chapter Twelve

Brad realized that the game had now changed with the marshal as an added hazzard. They were being watched by a man who was accustomed to watching, who knew the signs when matters were not going his way.

Talking the situation over with his two friends, and the new love in his life, Brad felt that action of some kind had to be taken.

They gathered in a restaurant to figure it out.

"Somebody," offered Stace, "has to keep an eye on Marshal Smith, as well as Comer and Ten."

"Well, we can all do that," suggested Gail.

"We'll have to do more," said Brad. "I want

to know where those Long Bar X cattle are and what's happening."

"So?" from Stace.

Brad glanced at Stace. "I think you and I had better go on a hunt, while you two," he added to Gail and Red, "stay in town to keep your eyes open."

"I'd like to go with you," Gail defended. "Three pairs of eyes are better than two."

"Four," added Red.

"I agree," Brad was tactful, "but also four bodies on horseback make a larger lump in the sage brush. Two can be less easily seen."

"We can split up," Gail was still defensive, "and have meeting places to talk over what we've learned."

A vision clouded Brad's mind, and he expressed it.

"And let the man with the scar get to you again?" He shook his head violently. "No way, girl, no way."

Gail, remembering, saw the point.

"So," she agreed, "Red and I will stay here, but Marshal Smith is sure to want to know where you two have gone."

"You can tell him we're still looking for EW cattle, and the GF brand as well, that we haven't given up the search yet."

Stace nodded. "He'll understand that."

Gail turned to Red. "How about it?"

Red was glum, but agreed.

Gail then turned to Brad and teased, "Does this mean that in our future together, I will always be the 'little woman,' who must stay home where it is safe and protected?"

Brad laughed. "You know better than that! What, me telling you what not to do? Oh, sure."

The humor in this brought some relief to the situation. Everybody relaxed. In fact, because a definite plan had been suggested, and passed on, the future was no longer a blank sky, but acquired some color in it. Hunger overtook them with a passion. They all ordered huge steaks with the trimmings, except for Red, who consumed two huge steaks with two slices of apple pie.

Early the next morning, so early the birds were still quietly nesting, Brad and Stace saddled up and left town. Brad gave Gail a special goodbye kiss after a quick breakfast, and she murmured, "Be careful. No bunch of cows is worth losing you."

Even though the birds were not yet up, Marshal Tom Smith was. He was still around, after a rough night in the saloons. He often thought the phase of the moon had something to do with human behavior. The fuller and brighter the moon, the goofier mankind, and last night the moon had shined like a giant, yellow orb in the black sky. The jail was full of drunks, and Smith was about to head for bed when he saw Brad and Stace.

Huh, he thought, *going to have to find out about that.*

"I got to admit," Brad said to Stace, "I just don't know where to look."

"Yeah, we've searched pretty well already."

"I don't think Comer would have headed them back to Newton yet."

"Railroad's not ready. Maybe in a couple months."

Brad tipped his broad-brimmed Stetson back, and sweat glistened on his forehead, though the sun was just finding day.

"Let's just look," he suggested. "We'll cover the same ground, but let's go farther inland."

They followed unmapped creeks and fringed the rolling hills. They camped in gullies so their fire would be hidden from sight. They ate hardtack and pemmican, washed down with coffee so hot it burned their eyes. Their horses were fed oats once a day, but for the rest, they foraged what grass there was available.

"Smoky, he don't relish this diet," remarked

Brad. "Hey, guy, when we get back to the barn it will be alfalfa, I promise."

And Smoky, as always when Brad spoke to him, waggled his ears.

The nights were long, and there was time to talk. Curious, Brad asked a delicate question one evening as diamond stars flashed in the sky.

"Why," Brad asked, "did you follow your, ah, fastest hand trade?"

Stace chucked another piece of greasewood on the fire. He sipped his coffee and scowled over its obstinate treachery. For a moment, Brad felt the flush of embarrassment. Maybe he'd gone too far into the man's privacy?

But Stace, throwing the dregs of his cup out, caught the moment. "I was young," he stated, "and stupid."

"We were all that, friend."

"Yeah, but I figured the way to an easy life was to get rich quick. I saw no harm in lifting cash from a bank now and then; after all, they had plenty. And now and then I helped lift payroll money from stages passing through."

"Sounds harmless." Brad was being sarcastic.

"Sure, but then I began to get challenged. Sometimes by members of the gang I happened to be with, and sometimes by some kid still green behind the ears in some saloon. And I saw I better get good with the smoking iron."

"I can see the kids after you began to get a reputation, but why the gang?"

"I always came in for the biggest cut. It was either that or I wouldn't play. I usually made the plans for bank robberies, looked the town over, figured the best time to hit, and learned the surest getaway routes. All that took time, and I cut myself in for more of the take."

"Pretty brave, considering the eager fellows you worked with."

"It didn't set good with them, for sure. So they questioned my authority, and I beat them to Old Judge Six Shooter."

"And that news spread, and gave you a reputation."

"And after that, the kids came into the act, so I practiced to be the best. I was a natural at both shooting straight and the fast draw. I didn't want to kill anybody, so I aimed to hurt. Sometimes I missed the hurt, though, which I regret."

"What landed you in jail?"

"I made the mistake of crossing the law, a deputy who had learned his trade from Pat Garret, you know the man who killed Billy the Kid? I was on the run after a good haul from an Arizona bank. Then I was cornered, and boxed up for three years. Those guys you saw me fighting wanted me back in the gang. And I said no. I had enough jail time, thanks." Stace then added, "All right, I gave you my life story. What about yours?"

Brad poured another cup of scalding brew and shrugged.

"What about me? I was Red fifteen years ago. Drifting about, getting into trouble like you. But then, Ed Warshal came along, and put me to work. I liked Ed. He was tough, and took no sass, but he taught me how to live right. Pretty simple, really."

"We should all have an Ed Warshal in our lives. You going to be one with Red?"

"You'd like that?"

"Sure, and you?"

"Yeah, he's a good kid. If I can give him a break, I will."

Stace smiled. "I like that, friend, I do."

While the pair were giving their biographies, brief though they were, things were happening elsewhere.

Fifty miles from Abilene, Slick Comer and Ten were at the site of the Long Bar X cattle. Both Brad and Stace had seen the trail thirty miles closer to town, but they had thought the herd was incoming, not outgoing. In the hardscrabble dirt, with two thousand milling animals, it wasn't always easy to tell which way was which.

Meanwhile, back in town, Marshal Tom Smith was mulling over Brad Tucker and Stace leaving town. He had already talked to Gail and Red, and had received the expected answer, that the two were trying to track the Long Bar X cattle. But Smith was suspicious. Why had they left town so quickly and so quietly, and why hadn't he been taken into their confidence?

A day after their departure, Marshal Smith told his deputies he was going to do some backtracking of his own. He would go alone, but he'd return in a couple of days.

In actuality, he was not tracking cattle. He knew where the Long Bar X cattle were. He was tracking Brad and Stace. He knew what they were up to, and he correctly guessed the direction they would take. He left town in the morning, and by noon, riding steadily, he had spotted them about two miles across the dry plains.

He had not been seen, so he stopped. There was no need to come closer. He had learned enough. As determined as the pair were, it was only a matter of time before they followed the right trail to the Long Bar X cattle. Comer and

Ten had to be warned. Marshal Smith didn't want anything to interfere with his future security or peace of mind.

While Smith considered his options, Gail received a visitor in Abilene. Ed was one of her hands from the GF ranch, and as long as she'd known him, since her childhood Ed had been showing her the secrets of good roping. He was now an assistant foreman, his duties consisting of taking care of the cattle not chosen for the drive and tending to the numerous daily chores of keeping a large ranch. Cowboys like Ed were also all-purpose repair men; they fixed barns and fences, cut a winter's supply of wood, rescued cattle who were stuck in bog holes, and tended to those who needed healing lineament on open sores.

But he couldn't repair everything on his own, so he had made haste for Abilene to speak with Gail.

"Gail," Ed said, "we need you back at the ranch. At least for a spell."

Gail had been delighted to see her friend and teacher, but was not surprised by the purpose of his visit. She had been expecting a messenger from the GF. She had known there were pressing matters back home, but had held off on returning.

"What," she asked warily, "is wrong, Ed?"

Ed was not a large man, but he was as wiry and tough as saddle leather. He grinned at the girl and held his hat in his hand as he spoke to her. It always amazed him to see this young, graceful woman taking charge. She used to be an awkward but determined child; how quickly things had changed!

"Well, Missy, you know we ain't exactly paper people back on the ranch. I can read all right, but I don't understand that stuff about money owed and all that."

"Are people getting anxious about their money?"

"Yes, ma'am, something like that. Bank people came out from Lisbon and said something about GF borrowing money for the drive up here."

"And they are worried?"

Ed nodded. "They appear to be so. So I said I'd get in touch with you, and here I am in touch."

He had the spice of humor in his words, and in spite of the seriousness of the situation, habit formed his sentences.

"All right." Gail reached over and put her hand on Ed's shoulder. "I'll come back, but I need just one more day, Ed. One more day. We are after the murderers who did this to the men and my father. I think we got them, but it'll take proof. Can I have one more day?"

"Sure. I'll rest over till tomorrow. You come back when you can."

She took Ed to supper, along with Red. The young boy and the older man hit it off well. Gail was pleased. If everything worked out as she hoped, and the mystery brought to a close, she would take Red back to the GF. He had proved himself. She wanted to give the boy a chance, and Ed would be a good boss.

Ed left the next morning with a promise from Gail that she'd return in one more day. After he left, she turned anxious eyes to the horizon. Where were Brad and Stace? They'd been gone four days and should have returned by now. She closed her mind to what might have happened, but she didn't for an instant underestimate the treacherous cunning of Ten, Slick Comer, or, possibly, the marshal.

She and Red took their places by the stockyards and both noticed that Marshal Smith was missing. Of course, as a lawman he could have many demands on his time. Gail considered this, but was suspicious anyway.

While she and Red were guessing what could have happened to Smith, Brad and Stace were closing in on the Long Bar X cattle. Somehow, on the afternoon of the third day out, they had stumbled almost smack into the center of the missing herd. The two had stopped to water their horses at a small stream, and while the animals stuck their snouts into the cool water, there was silence in the world, no creaking saddles, no hoof sounds striking the difficult earth, but into this silence came the restless sounds of cattle.

Brad and Stace were at the base of a riffle of hills, not so far from the top as to discourage walking up the incline. They dismounted, tied their mounts to clumps of sage brush, and started on foot. Stace, more accustomed to stealth than Brad, cautioned him.

"Boulder to boulder," he whispered, "our best friend is the shade. Keep your eyes open. If the cattle are there, guards will be posted."

Darting piecemeal up the slope, hidden partly by tall brush as well as the boulders, they crested the top crouching, and they were rewarded. Stretched out in a shallow valley was the Long Bar X brand. The cattle's bellows and grunts could now be easily heard, and among the critters were a couple dozen men, some on horses, others waiting by a half a dozen fires.

"They're changing the brand," Brad squinted, "looks like a bar and a double X. See it?"

"Yeah, and I see more than that."

Brad then saw what Stace was talking about. Slick Comer, Ten, and Marshal Tom Smith were all standing around together in a huddle.

"Well, well," said Brad.

"Yeah." Stace suddenly started to his feet, fingering the butt of his pistol. "It's time to settle." His voice was steel.

Brad quickly reached up and pulled him down behind the covering brush.

"What are you doing?" he hissed.

"Time to settle with some people who need settling—lying marshals, smooth cattle rustlers, would-be gunmen. Let go of me."

But Brad tightened his grip. "Are you crazy? We wouldn't fire five shots before we'd be cut down by about two dozen men."

"Those five shots would be worth it."

"You do that, and we'll be the bad guys. There's not a man in this mess who wouldn't swear we started the fight and cut down a federal marshal."

"Are you saying we won't be solving anything?"

"Not the right thing."

"Being?"

"I want them to bring those new-branded cows to Abilene. I think I can also show what happened to the GF and EW brand. There'll be a showdown then, Stace. The right time, the right place."

"You sure?"

"Nothing is for sure in this life," was the ironic reply, "but I think so. Yes."

"You fancy that woman, Gail, don't you?"

The sudden change of subject threw Brad off for a moment.

"Huh?"

Stace grinned. "Don't give me that 'huh' stuff. It's written all over you like ripples on a sand dune."

"Huh, well, ah, yes, sure, I guess so."

"Guess so?" Stace allowed a wide grin. "You are in up to your neck."

"Look, can we talk about this later?"

"Yeah, guess we better get out of here."

"Let's go." Brad did some quick mental arithmetic. "I figure they got maybe eight hundred, a thousand head to brand yet. They'll show up in town somewhere between ten days and two weeks."

"Close enough," agreed Stace. "We'll be waiting, eh?"

"Oh, yes. We'll be waiting."

Chapter Thirteen

On seeing Brad Tucker and Stace depart town, Marshal Tom Smith was confronted with some serious, and dangerous, thinking.

Knowing Stace was a Pinkerton agent and that Tucker was going to remain relentless until he avenged his men, Smith realized that, along with Slick Comer and Ten, they were on a overloaded tree branch. One wriggle, one squirm the wrong way, and down they would all fall.

He had to contact Comer and Ten, and he was the only one who could do it. The kind of talk they were going to have could not come from his deputies. Look what had happened to Waddy!

The fifty mile trip to where the Long Bar X

stock was being rebranded was not an easy one. There were many low hills, brush scrabble, rocky plains, and little water, but Smith knew the way. He even knew some shortcuts.

Halfway to his destination, he saw Brad Tucker and Stace. They did not see him, as he ducked into an arroyo, once enlivened by a small river, but now dry. He waited, scarcely breathing; if he were discovered he would have to have a handy excuse for being there.

The moments passed into a quarter of an hour. Dismounting, he crept to the edge of the arroyo and found that the way was clear. The pair had disappeared, and since they were heading in the opposite direction, he was safe. Still, one never knew what direction a search party might take. The pair could have doubled back, they could have even seen him, but the way was clear for the moment.

He mounted and headed for his destination. His mind was troubled. Should he warn Comer and Ten about the two? They would immediately hunt them down. They'd take a dozen men on the hunt so as to be sure not to miss. Stace was, so he'd heard, deadly, and might take a few with him, but he'd be killed and so would Tucker.

That would be the safest route to follow, but as he drew closer to his destination, his mind clouded with the memory of Waddy, his deputy getting shot in cold blood. That did not set well with Marshal Tom Smith. He knew what he was doing when he entered a partnership with Comer and Ten; he realized they were killers who killed freely and without conscience, but when they hit his own man, he started to take exception.

He didn't like himself for what had happened, however, he managed to keep his attention focused; the net result was what counted. He now had a good amount in a Newton bank, a comfortable sum. With his cut from the Long Bar X sale, he could get out of the business altogether. There was a ranch near Lisbon that he would have enough money to purchase outright. The Long Bar X sale would add a comfortable cushion to his accounts.

When he arrived, Slick Comer and Ten were concerned that he had absented himself from Abilene for several days. Wouldn't people suspect something fishy? What about his deputies? Why not send one of them? They became openly hostile to Smith, who assured them that he'd explained to his staff that he wanted a long look. He explained that the killing of Waddy gave him the excuse he needed, that it was a personal matter, and that people understood.

But neither Ten nor his boss, Comer, would

let it go. A tension rose among the three, raising invisible hackles along the back of the marshal's neck. He had long been a person of authority, in charge, and he didn't like being an outsider, a second-rater. He had planned to tell about seeing Tucker and Stace. He had planned on more than that. The woman, Gail, and the boy, Red, should also be eliminated. All four should be silenced. Men must be sent to hunt them down. Dead, there would be no chance of a slipup. He could, himself, help take care of Miss Fanchy and the boy. Who would suspect him? He had the reputation of being a straight-forward, no-nonsense lawman. He was beyond reproach.

But as these thoughts crossed his mind, something else, deep down, started to confuse the usual clarity of his thinking. What was he doing? He was glibly advocating the deaths of four people. He, who protected life, was promoting killing. For all of his days he had hated killers, hunted them down, and rejoiced in their captures. What had he become? Was he really like Comer and Ten? Such thoughts were against everything the marshal was supposed to stand for.

He endured the chiding, and anger of Comer and Ten, but as he did so, he made a complete turnabout in his thinking. He didn't want any more killing. Thirty or more men had been slaughtered during the rustlings, and that was too many!

And so, without a word to his associates, Marshal Smith left for the return trip to Abilene. He said nothing about seeing Tucker and Stace, nor did he mention anything about doing away with the girl or the boy. His hackles still up, his dignity ruffled, feeling more on the fringe instead of a solid member of the gang, he kept his mouth shut.

Chapter Fourteen

Gail had promised Ed she'd return after one more day. That day passed, dragged actually, without a sign of either Brad or Stace.

The girl grew restless. Even Red, as young as he was and not prone to reading adults very well yet sensed her inner turmoil.

"Is there anything I can do?" he asked. "You want me to go find Stace and Mr. Tucker?"

The girl shook her head quickly.

"No," she softened, "I'm sorry, Red. Does it show that much?"

"Miss Fanchy, Gail, if I might, yes," he smiled with the romance of it, "it does. You miss him quite a bit, don't you?"

"They are both on a dangerous mission,

Red. Yes," she took his hand, "yes, I miss him. I want them back safely."

Red squeezed the hand, a bit surprised at how tough the skin was; she seemed so soft otherwise.

"Don't worry," he assured her without any authority to do so, "they'll be okay. Stace," he added with pride, "can handle himself—and so can Mr. Tucker, I'm sure."

He had no sooner uttered those prophetic words, than the two arrived in town. Gail and Red saw them walking their horses toward a stable. Gail ran out to greet them. Brad leaned over in the saddle and swooped her up in front of him.

He kissed her without hesitation or ceremony in front of the onlookers. She wrapped her arms around him and murmured, "Thank heaven you're back safely."

Red grinned from the sidelines, and called, "See, Gail, I told you so!"

Stace, also smiling, declared, "Wow, what a greeting. I ain't never seen any better."

After the horses had been lodged, and both Brad and Stace had washed trail dust out of their hair, the four found a restaurant table.

Over steaks, Gail and Red were informed about what had taken place.

"Then those scoundrels do have the Long

Bar X brand! We know that for sure now!" was Gail's violent response. "We better tell the marshal right away."

Brad shook his head in the negative, and told her what he and Stace and seen.

Gail was shocked.

"That good man!" she exclaimed. "Whatever happened to him?"

"My one guess is money," Stace said. "Smith wants it, and has made a bargain with the devil."

"Two devils," agreed Gail. "So what do we do?"

"There's nothing we can do right now. If we went to the town leaders, would they believe us? Smith has been a trusted man for a long time around here."

"And," Red added, "we are newcomers, after all."

There was a silence, which Brad broke with, "Let's just wait. If my scheme works, it'll all come to light—in a flash, I might add."

"You're not going to tell us, are you?" Gail pressed his hand. "Why not?"

"Let's just say 'because,' and let it go at that."

"Quite a bit of trust on that 'because.'"

"Yes. But go along, all three of you. It could be worth it."

They had another cup of coffee, and then Gail brought up another matter.

"How long," she asked, "before the first Long Bar X—or Bar Double X—gets here?"

Brad ventured an educated guess, "Maybe ten days. Why?"

She then told about Ed's visit.

"I am going to have to go home to straighten the paperwork out."

"Paperwork?" Stace was puzzled. In his entire life, he had never been bothered by such a matter.

Gail smiled. "Sometimes, a person gets caught in it like a trap, and you have to do something to get free."

Stace nodded, but understood nothing.

Brad interrupted. "So when do you leave?"

"Tomorrow at the latest, but I want to be here when the showdown comes. I need that."

"How far is it to Lisbon?"

"Maybe a hundred and fifty miles."

"Three hundred down and back."

Gail smiled. "Yes, dear, that's what it adds up to."

"We should get started right now, today."

"We?" Gail looked at him. "We?"

"If you think I'm going to let you go alone, think again, girl. Marshal Smith could tip off his buddies, and they'd come looking. No, I'm going, and that's final."

"I was hoping you'd say that."

She kissed him.

"We'll go too," offered Stace, "Red and me."

"Somebody has to keep an eye open here," Brad reminded him.

"Tucker's Law?" It was Stace's turn to grin.

"Yeah, something like that."

Stace nodded. "Fine, but ten days, no more. I want to see what you have up your sleeve."

Stace realized, too, there would be more than a trick. If Brad was successful in showing Comer, Ten, and, now, Smith to be crooks, he would be doing his own job as a Pinkerton man. There was sure to be a confrontration between him and Ten, and he wanted that. It no longer mattered whether Comer paid him.

Brad and Gail left that night under a full moon. They followed the road, hazarding no shortcuts. The long way would most likely be the shortest. After three days driving hard, they arrived at the ranch ten miles south of Lisbon. Their horses were tired and Smoky's ears hardly waggled when Brad spoke to him. They'd rest up until the return trip. In the meantime, the GF string would be used.

Along the way from Abilene, there was

plenty of time for talk, and Gail explained the odd setup of one of the GF's financial setups.

Over a campfire and coffee, she said, "My father wanted his men, especially the long-time employees, to have a comfortable retirement. There comes a time in every cowboy's life when he simply has to quit. This is rough work, as you know. In the course of a lifetime, bones are broken, backs give out, sickness takes a toll—once the mumps nearly knocked all the crew out for a couple of weeks. Eventually, a man has to get out of the business."

Brad nodded. He had found much the same at the EW. Bodies wore out.

"So what Dad did was deposit money in the bank for each man who had been with the GF more than five years. And each year, after the stock had been sold, he added a percentage of the sale price to each man's account."

"How long has this been going on?"

"For at least twenty years. The men you will meet at the ranch have all been with us that long."

Brad gave a low whistle. "Must be quite a windfall."

Gail agreed. "Dad wanted each man to have enough so he wouldn't have to worry. Each one would get the cash and a couple of acres for a cabin. I have to make sure that money is safe."

"That alone is a good reason for the trip. Glad you explained." He kissed her. "Your father was quite a man."

"Yes," said the girl quietly, "he was, and I miss him very much."

Suddenly she burst out. "Those savages who killed him! I want to see them hung, Brad. Hung!"

Tears came, and Brad drew her close.

"I'll do my best to see to that," he promised gently, "or something final for them, you can be sure."

The GF spread was typical of the style in the region. A big house for the family, and bunkhouses for the men, two in the case of the GF. There were corrals, two barns, a tool shed, and outhouses. Everything was in place, and there was a place for everything. A small stream supplied water for daily use, but there was also a dug well. Much the same, Brad noted, as the EW ranch. Functional. No trim, but functional.

There were six men in the crew, four hands, including Ed, a cook, and a bullcook—the man who took care of the daily upkeep of the ranch. They had all been with the GF for twenty years or more.

Ed, who had handled the finances for the ranch while Gail was gone, admitted he had gone as far as he could go.

"I paid the horse feed bill, new lumber for bunkhouse number one's west wall—remember it got partly ripped during a storm last winter. Also I paid for a new stall in one of the barns, paid the men's, wages, and kept up with other things, but there's one expense we can't handle."

"Which is?" Prompted Gail.

"Well, your Daddy, he borrowed seven thousand to get the herd to Abilene. He'd have sold for a good price, and paid the borrowing off. But," Ed stopped, and stared at Gail, "well, girl, you know what happened. I'm so sorry, but the GF is broke. That's why I came for you. I don't know what to do about it."

Neither do I, thought Gail, but she expressed confidence.

"I'll go see the banker today, Ed. Surely, we can work something out. The GF has got a good reputation."

Brad went with her. There was nothing much he could do except offer support. Ed Warshal took care of EW expenses himself, except for daily needs. The big money stuff didn't reach Brad.

The banker, Mr. John Richardson, greeted

Gail like she was his daughter. They were friends of long standing. He had watched her grow from a baby to a lovely, and capable, young woman.

"I'm sorry about this," he said, and Brad realized the man was sincere, "but my hands are tied, Gail. Your father and I signed a contract, which was approved by the bank's board of directors. Perhaps, if only I was the only one involved, the loan could be stretched out for another six months, but as it is . . ."

"I see."

Gail tried to be smooth about it, but she felt anything but smooth inside.

"Perhaps we can get an extension long enough to sell the rest of the cattle, John, and pay off the debt in part, anyway."

"We have talked about that, the board and I—nobody likes this, Gail, and we tried to figure out ways for the GF to settle, but if you sell the rest of the stock, that wouldn't cover half of the debt, and the GF would still go into receivership."

"Meaning?"

"Putting it bluntly, you'd be broke, bankrupt."

"Damn," said Gail indelicately.

"Exactly," agree John Richardson. Then he added, "We aren't Simon Legrees here, Gail. We'll work with you on this. We will have to take over, but we can keep you and your men on for at least awhile. We won't turn you out into the cold."

"But, bottom line is?"

"The GF will belong to the bank, and subject to a sale to anybody who can afford the price. My hope, then, is you'd be kept on as manager."

"Not exactly a bright future," murmured Gail. "No indeed."

On the ride back to the ranch, Brad ventured with, "I wouldn't have thought seven thousand was that much."

Gail shook her head.

"Around here it is. Ranchers in this region are not big—like the EW, yours. You have thousands of acres of open range. You can easily handle ten thousand cattle. We are limited, because range grass is not plentiful."

"So, when roundup time comes, what you sell is bread and butter?"

"Basically, yes. We aren't rich, Brad. Comfortable, but we don't have that much money in reserve. We go from year to year." Then she added with bitterness. "We'd have been fine except for—well, you know what."

"I know," he responded quietly, "I know."

He leaned over from his horse and kissed her, and at the same time resolved, more deeply than ever, to get the ones who did this to her, and to all of them.

At the ranch, Ed was told about the sinking circumstances.

"I thought it might be something like that," Ed's lined face took on sympathy. "Sure sorry about it, Gail."

"We'll work something out," the girl said. "You won't lose your job."

Brad interrupted with, "Maybe I can get Warshal to get into this. He's always looking for a new range."

Gail brightened. "Maybe?"

"Won't hurt to ask. He trusts my judgement."

They were in the kitchen. The cook had made coffee and was getting the fixings for lunch. He was a large man, with sloping shoulders, bare, clean arms, and a kindly face. He had been with the GF for twenty-one years, and wouldn't "work noplace else on this here green earth."

All the men, the long timers, as well as the short timers, felt the same way. The GF treated their crews with dignity and fairness.

Ed took a sip of his brew, gave Gail a thoughtful look, and then said, "Missy, me and the boys have another plan you might want to hear."

"Always ready, Ed, always."

"Well, we got that money in the bank in our name. You know, the fund your father set up for us years ago."

"Yes. I've been going to talk to you about that. The money is secure, Ed. It's in the names of everybody involved, individual accounts."

Ed nodded. "We been checking, and Mr. Richardson told us about the amounts and all." His eyes were wide with surprise, and delight. "Gail, thanks to your Daddy, we are rich."

Gail smiled. "I'm so glad. And that two acres for each man, that's already been settled. The acres are registered in your names. Nobody else can get them."

"You could always depend on your father, but," he hesitated, "well, let me tell you what the boys and I have in mind." He stood up, a bit nervous, but also determined.

"Well, we got over ten thousand combined in the bank. Why don't we give you the money to pay off the debts?"

Gail was silent. She was not prepared for the offer, and it hit her right in the heart. She remained silent until Ed prompted her with, "Missy? What do you think?"

In the meantime, Brad sat quietly. This was not the time for him to chip in. This was the time for Gail and her crew to talk.

"Why, Ed," Gail's voice was calm enough,

but her heart was racing, "Ed, what can I say? The GF would pay you back with big interest. What can I say? I just don't know!"

"Well, we'll make it a business deal. We can get a lawyer, or Mr. Richardson, or, heck, just a handshake between you and us. What we'll get is a part of the ranch. We each of us come in for a percentage of whatever profits there are, but you'll be the boss." He glanced at the cook. "Right, Cookie?"

And the cook, wiping his hands on a fold of cotton sack cloth nodded, grinned, and said, "You betcha, Gail. You betcha."

All at once the offer sunk in, and Gail leaped up from her chair. "Do you mean that for a share of the ranch, you'll do that, Ed? All of you together?"

"This is our home, Missy. It's where we belong. Yes, we'll help you in this fight. Like Cookie says, you betcha."

Gail swept around the table and hugged Ed in a giant bear hug, and then kissed him on the cheek.

"Yes, by all means! We can keep the ranch in the family. Oh, good heavens! Let's get the other men in, and talk." She turned. "Cookie, get out your pie plates and put more coffee on. We got some deciding to do."

In the space of the rest of the day, the matter

was made legal by the banker, John Richardson. The papers were notorized and placed in a vault.

From not knowing where to turn, a turn had been made for Gail Fanchy. And it was good.

Chapter Fifteen

The next morning, Brad approached Gail with an idea. He had been thinking it over since they'd left Abilene, five days before. The idea seemed good to him, but he hesitated. He'd only known Gail for a short time. They were not that well acquainted, were they? Wouldn't she be offended? Or maybe feel rushed?

But the day after the GF ranch became the property of seven people, he felt that he'd grab the toe of the sock and plunge ahead. The time had come.

They had had breakfast in the mess hall with the rest of the men. After the meal was over, and the dishes put in the sink, Brad invited Gail for a walk.

"Let's go see old Smoky. He got pretty tired on the way over, and I want to know if he's ready for the return trip. We rode both horses pretty hard."

"There was a reason," Gail reminded him, "we had to get here and back to Abilene in time for whatever comes next."

"We better leave tomorrow."

"Yes. Now, what did you want to talk about?"

It wasn't very romantic, Brad remembered later, but, at the time, his words seemed like the embodiment of romance itself.

"Will you," he said, "marry me?"

The girl, who was scooping up a pitchfork full of hay for Smoky, paused.

"What?"

"I said, will you marry me?"

"I thought you said something like that."

"Well, will you?"

"When?"

"Today." Brad glanced at his watch. "It is now seven A.M. Let's get married this morning and head on back to Abilene today."

"You make it seem so cut and dried. Like you were shopping for oats."

"Well, I never done this before, and I guess I'm not very good at it."

"I expected you would have a candlelight

dinner for me when you proposed, and violins playing softly."

"Well . . ." Then Brad realized the girl was teasing him.

She went to him and kissed him fully on the lips.

"I thought," she said, looking into eyes which reflected her own deep love, "you'd never ask."

He hugged her to him, felt her body soft in the right places, yielding, yet with a compliance given rarely if ever at all.

"I'm a dumb cowboy," he murmured, "but we all do the best we can. I don't have much to offer, Gail, but maybe I can buy a piece of the GF." He grinned. "I don't want to be thought of as a 'kept man.' "

"That'll be the day."

Gail rested her head against his chest.

"I thank God I met you. Out of a terrible tragedy, something lovely has happened. I'll always be grateful for that."

He kissed her.

"Let's go find a preacher or somebody who can marry us."

There were preachers in Lisbon. Three of them actually, Presbyterian, Baptist, and Catholic, but the pair decided on a civil wedding.

There just wasn't the time for a formal ceremony.

A magistrate married them at twelve noon. The witnesses were the crew of the GF, and the banker with his wife.

After the ceremoney, Brad treated everyone to a wedding lunch in town. Because of the suddenness of the wedding, there had been no time to plan for festivities, but the restaurant did pretty well. There were baked sage hens, mashed potatos, a salad of greens freighted from Abilene by wagon, and a cake, hurriedly whipped up by the cook who had been camp cook on trail drives and knew how to make do very well. What was more, dinner was on the house because the cook, a man by the name of Pete, had also known Gail Fanchy from childhood.

"With my blessings, Missy," he told her, throwing in a kiss on the cheek to boot. "Best of luck to both of you."

The GF crew made much of the newlyweds, and Ed promised to keep things in line, until the couple returned.

"Be careful, sweetheart," he told her, "but get those you-know-whats who did this terrible thing. We all of us here back you with our hearts, bodies, and souls. Send for us if we can help."

Gail, touched by the attention, tried not to weep. She didn't want to be a sissy, she told herself, but she wept anyway, and the crew was delighted, and wept with her, and a damn good time was had by all.

The trip back took three days, driving the horses hard, fifty miles a day. Neither Brad nor Gail noticed the time. Wrapped in the glow and flow of love, they could have climbed the Rockies and thought the ground flat. If Smoky and the other horse, an animal from the GF string, lagged a bit, and if Smokey's ears didn't waggle so heartily when Brad spoke to him, the humans did not notice the fatigue. They were not cruel, just in love and oblivious to the world.

As soon as they reached town, the horses were housed in a warm barn, watered by the help, and fed oats and alfalfa hay. The weary animals sighed heavily and relaxed.

Brad and Gail checked in at the hotel, then looked for Stace and Red. The two were at the corrals watching events.

When they saw the newly married couple approaching, Brad said quickly and quietly to Gail, "Don't mention the wedding. Let's have a bit of fun, do you mind?"

Gail shook her head. Brad could have said,

"Let's dance naked in the street," and she'd have agreed.

"About time you got back," Stace said. "The Long Bar X cattle are on the move. We was afraid you'd be late, or maybe got caught by Ten and Comer, and—well, you know."

"We know," Brad responded. "But we didn't have any problems that way."

"Is everything alright at the GF?" Red wanted to know.

He was starting a beard, and it showed up black on his chin, even though he was red haired. He stroked the thin hairs thoughtfully.

"We missed you," Brad said simply. "Ain't been the same without all four of us together."

"Glad we made it on time," said Gail. Turning to Stace, she asked, "So what's the plan?"

"Just wait, I guess." Stace nodded at Brad, "He's the man with the plan. What you got in mind, or is it still a secret?"

There was just a hint of sarcasm in Stace's voice.

"It still is," came the blunt reply. Then with a change in tone, "What about our friends? Are they in town, or out rustling another herd someplace?"

Stace shook his head. "I doubt if they'll try that until the Long Bar X stock is sold off. I think the next job they pull will be closer to

Newton. Comer, Ten, and the marshal have been here the whole time."

As they were speaking, the three men appeared on the scene. They were involved with a fourth man, recognized as a buyer.

"They got Jones," observed Brad, "he'll deal with anything that moves, no questions asked."

"Crooked?" from Gail.

"As a dog's hind leg, but nothing could ever be proved." Brad smiled. "That is about to change."

Stace was curious. "Is that your secret? You know how to show him up, and the others too?"

"Something like that," was the elusive response.

"How?" Red was forthright in his innocence.

"You'll find out—I hope," was the enigmatic reply.

Comer, Ten, Jones, and the marshal were closing in on the corral where Brad and the others were.

"Well," Stace said gently, "how do you do?"

He addressed Ten directly, ignoring the others. Here was a man he had been asked to kill by Comer. He would never collect now, but the confrontration would take place for other reasons.

Ten stiffened.

"I do fine," he returned with an equally soft voice. "Who is asking?"

"I'm called Stace. Surely, you know?"

Ten nodded. "Yes, I know."

Both men were facing each other, each wondering if there was enough excuse to draw, then deciding there was not. No insults had been exchanged; all was, on the surface, normal, just two men exchanging greetings. Only those in the surrounding group understood what was going on; Two of the fastest draws in the country were testing the ground.

Dislike burned in Ten's eyes, and the same could be said of Stace. Both knew that sooner or later there would be a showdown. Pride was as much a factor as anything in this inevitable contest. Stace, in spite of his time in jail, in spite of his Pinkerton connection, in spite of his resolution to follow the straight and narrow, was, nevertheless, a man with old habits, and the kind of status very few achieve as a top gunman.

Ten was the same breed, but quite a bit more. Stace had never killed, except in self-defense. Ten killed anybody who was likely to disrupt his plans.

Marshal Smith, knowing exactly what was going on in the two prideful minds, also knew this was not the time for a match. Let the two face each other some other day, but not now. Tomorrow, the sale of the newly branded Long

Bar X, now the Bar Double X, was starting. He wanted no interference with the sale. He planned to retire after this job, and a killing would only complicate the proceedings.

He said to Comer, breaking the tension, "Where's Jones?"

The man had disappeared. He would come back the next day. There was a lot riding on the purchase for him.

The marshal then moved along, sort of shoving Ten with him.

Ten glared back at Stace, who returned the fiery glare.

Red was looking at Stace with deep admiration. Though the boy didn't know the full ramifications of this confrontration, he knew this much: Stace had not backed down before and he wouldn't now, even to a cold-blooded killer like Ten. Red's whole being trembled with respect for what he saw as bare-boned courage.

"What time is the first of your stock coming?" Brad called to Comer.

Without time to think of an evasive answer, the reply came, "Oh, early tomorrow, I guess."

Brad nodded, and the four left the corral. They had no reason to linger.

They spent the rest of the day talking over events at the GF ranch. Gail explained how the missing cattle had almost ruined her company.

Brad explained how the crisis was met by the crew, and also by Gail's father. Had it not been for him, there wouldn't have been any money.

They broke up about ten in the evening and headed for their rooms. It was then that Brad, with Gail's full permission, did his thing.

When they arrived at Gail's room, he went in with her, bidding Stace and Red a pleasant goodnight at the doorway.

When they were safely inside, Gail whispered, "That was mean."

"Yeah. Well, it will give them something to think about for sure."

Gail laughed.

Brad also laughed.

And the amazed pair still standing in the hall heard the laughter, and Stace said, "Well, what do you know?"

Red said, "You never really do know, do you?"

"It was a long trip to Lisbon, I guess."

"Longer that we thought."

Chapter Sixteen

The next morning, the newlyweds showed up at breakfast to meet Stace and Red. The other two came in next, and sat carefully in their chairs. Neither was able to face Brad or Gail directly. Stace talked about the weather, and how hot it would get that day. Red spoke about Smoky, whom he had visited in the barn earlier.

"He's getting plenty of eats. The trip to, ah, Lisbon kind of wore him out."

Gail produced a piece of paper, and slid it across to Stace. Stace, startled, glanced at the paper, then glanced at it again. He picked it up, read it, and passed it to Red. The boy also scanned it, and both man and boy grinned widely.

"And you let us think . . ." said Red.

"That was pretty low," added Stace.

"A marriage certificate," said Red.

"And you let us think . . ." repeated Stace, and his grin deepened. "Man, you had us going, I gotta say that!"

Red was delighted. He looked at Stace.

"We have to celebrate. Let's buy them breakfast."

Stace agreed, but went one better.

"This evening, after this day is over, we'll find the best meal in town for them." The waiter had brought coffee, and Stace hoisted his in a toast, "Best of luck to you both."

Red raised his cup as well. "Yes," he was still in joy, "yes all the way."

Then Brad came to the serious matter, the one they were all there for, the one that would either make fools of them or hang a bunch of thieves.

"We better get to the corrals," he said quietly, "quite a bit depends on what happens next."

Slick Comer, Ten, Marshal Smith, and the buyer, Jones, were ahead of them. Sierra and several others of the gang were also present.

"That's him," exlaimed Gail, pointing.

"He's one of them who got into my room that time!"

"I seen him before," said Red. "He was at that soddy when Ten killed the deputy marshal."

All at once, the mood was turning somber. What had been a jolly breakfast was not leading into a jolly day.

Stace headed for Sierra, but Brad pulled him back.

"Let's not have trouble like that—not yet. The time has not come, not yet."

A tall man in a gray business suit, white shirt, black tie, and tailored boots approached them.

He opened courteously in a well-spoken eastern college accent, "Are you," he addressed Gail, "connected with the GF ranch?"

"I am." She was curious. "And you?"

"I represent the Long Bar X people."

He produced a business card, and handed it to Gail The card read:

Michael Hull, Attorney at Law
Specializing in Misappropriation

Gail handed the card to the others.

After reading it, Brad asked, "What does this word mean, 'misappropriation'?"

"We investigate such things as rustling large

herds, shady water practices, piggish range hogs, and matters like that. I represent the owners of the Long Bar X ranch."

He took in Brad. "I take it you are connected with the lost EW herd?"

"Yes. How would you know these things?"

The answer was blunt. "I ask questions."

Then Michael Hull added, "There is a reward of ten thousand dollars to whoever uncovers the rascals who killed the Long Bar X men and took two thousand head of cattle."

"That," Stace observed, "is a sizeable amount."

"It was a sizeable crime."

"Well," Brad said, "stick around, the answer is coming along pretty quick."

On the other side of the corral, Ten, Comer, and the marshal were watching the man in the suit.

"Who is he supposed to be?" Ten wanted to know. He was suspicious of anything, or anybody, not known to him.

"He is an investigator," Marshal Smith told him. "He stopped at the office a couple of days ago and told me he was looking into the Long Bar X rustle."

Slick Comer laughed quietly.

"I wish him luck. Here the cattle are right under his nose, and he will never know it."

There was a grunt of approval from the others, though Ten's grunt was not so firm as it could have been.

It was now Brad's turn to put his money were his mouth was.

He stood near the gate where the Bar Double X cattle were being herded. Jones, the buyer, was counting.

"Say," Brad opened, "how much you paying for these beefs?"

"Who wants to know?"

"I got me a considerable bunch coming in."

Jones brightened. "Twenty a head, depending."

"Good enough."

He handed Jones a twenty dollar bill.

"That one's mine," he said, pointing to a critter who was just about to enter.

Pulling his pistol, he shot the beef between the eyes.

"Sorry," he muttered, "this has got to be done."

The animal fell heavily to the ground, kicked once, and lay still in death.

There was a startled silence in the crowd that had gathered. Ten, Comer, the marshal, and Sierra were transfixed. Brad's own group was not much better, and others simply stared.

Had the man gone crazy?

Brad quickly withdrew a long sheath knife from its scabbard. He had sharpened it at the blacksmith shop to an edge he could shave with. Without hesitation, he skinned out the brand, and held up the skin inside out.

There, in plain sight, was the Long Bar X brand, dried, and set from long healing. But another slant across the bar was obviously very fresh. It was still bloody, and not in the least dried hard.

"There it is!" cried Brad. "You can all see that the old brand, the Long Bar X has been changed to the Bar XX."

Ten screamed at Slick Comer, "You piece of filth! You told me these were honest cattle!"

It was a wise move that only Ten could have thought of so quickly. Pass the blame at once.

Comer was wearing his pistol, something he did not do often while in town. "You're in this as deep as I am," he cried, and pulled his weapon.

Ten shot him through the heart.

Sierra, then sprung into action. He might have been an outlaw, a killer, and accustomed to narrow escapes, but this time he realized there would be no escape.

He had seen Gail, and now shouted at her, "You're to blame! I shoulda kilt you when I had the chance."

He drew his pistol, and aimed it at her, but

was stopped with a shot from Marshal Tom Smith.

"Maybe," cried the lawman, "I can right some of the wrong I've done by this!"

Sierra dropped, but, he squeezed off one more shot, and Smith died on the spot.

That left Brad, Stace, and Ten facing each other.

But Brad didn't want to have anything to do with it.

The matter had shifted to Stace and Ten, and the two faced each other, almost happily.

"Now we'll see," said Ten.

Two shots roared out, one—two, as loud as thunder and as fast as lightning.

Ten jerked stiff, and an expression of surprise passed over his face. He looked long at Stace, then his .44 tumbled from nerveless fingers, and he crumpled.

Stace was hit in the chest. He lay on the ground on his back looking up into the sky. He knew he'd been mortally hit.

Red dashed to his side, and cradled the man's head in his lap.

"Stace," he said, "Stace, don't do it, don't go out on me. Don't go."

And Stace, outlaw, Pinkterton man, and ex-con, gazed up at the young face hovering so close to his.

"It's my time," he whispered in what voice he had left, "so don't grieve for me." He was silent, then whispered again, "is he dead?"

Red knew whom he meant, and nodded.

"Then I beat him, eh? He died first."

Even as close to the grave as he was, the matter was important to him.

"Listen, kid," Red drew closer, "do two things for me."

"Anything, Stace."

"Shave off that silly beard, and pay attention to Brad and Gail. Any money I get from the reward is yours."

By this time, Brad and Gail were at Stace's side. They heard his last words, and the three bowed their heads when their friend and associate breathed his last.

Red wept without shame. He was learning a great and hard lesson about life. Only an hour or two earlier, they were laughing at breakfast about the trick that Gail and Brad had played on them. They were planning a celebration to take place that very evening. Then, quite suddenly, tragedy had struck, and lives were changed forever. Stace had passed from Red's life forever, and there was nothing he could do to change that.

The silence that came over the place was eerie. Four bodies lay in their final position, forever still. One man later said the scene reminded him of the battle at Gettysburg, where he'd served in the Union Army. After the last gun had sounded, there were bodies from both the north and southern sides scattered around like wheat straws.

Others would forever wonder at Marshal Smith's last words, as Sierra's bullet took his life, "Maybe I can right some of the wrongs I've done . . ."

Even his deputies, those closest to him, never guessed about Marshal Smith's dark side. Nor was anybody left, who counted, who would tell. The rest of Slick Comer's gang discretely vanished.

Epilogue

Michael Hull made good on his statement. He handed over a cashier's check for ten thousand dollars.

"It is to be divided equally," he directed, "among all of you, including the estates of Stace and the marshal."

The three debated about the 'marshal' part of the deal, but Tom Smith was regarded as a hero by Abilene folks. He had caught the bad ones and jailed them many times, and he had saved the life of the girl, Miss Fanchy, from the gun of outlaw Sierra.

At Brad's suggestion, who would always be thankful that the marshal's aim had been true, the trio let it be. Smith's money was spent on a statue of him, as approved by the city's chiefs.

Stace was buried in the town cemetery, and a marble headstone read, "Here Lies a Man, And His Name Was Stace."

Brad, Gail, and Red returned to the GF ranch. Brad resigned his position with the EW people. Ed Warshal, to show his appreciation for Brad's part in solving the murders, and rustling, gave his ex-foreman a sizeable share of stock in Warshal enterprises. These grew considerably in value. Along with their own hard work, and success with the GF, life became comfortable, if not wealthy. It was enough.

As life rolled the years by, Gail and Brad had four children, two boys and two girls. The boys, after learning ranch life from the bottom up, found their interests pointed in other directions. They made names for themselves in politics and business, though they returned home often for visits.

The girls also became adept at ranching and were a force in keeping things running smoothly.

Red, whose real name was Franklin Lassiter, shaved his beard. In an age where beards were considered manly, he never tried for another. He would be forever grateful to three people who had taken a runaway under wing and gave him direction—Brad, Gail, and, of course, a man who would, always, remain a hero to him, Stace.

In the evenings, Brad and Gail would sometimes find chairs on the porch and watch the evening sun turn the sky on fire. Gail would take her husband's hand in her own, and whisper "TUCKER'S LAW." The two would smile at each other, and remember those brave days.